ENCHANTED - THE WEDDING STORY

The Sugar Maple Chronicles - Book 5

BARBARA BRETTON

Free Spirit Press

Praise for Barbara Bretton

"Bretton's characters are always real and their conflicts believable."
— *Chicago Sun-Times*

"Soul warming... A powerful relationship drama [for] anyone who enjoys a passionate look inside the hearts and souls of the prime players."
— Midwest Book Review

"[Bretton] excels in her portrayal of the sometimes sweet, sometimes stifling ties of a small community. The town's tight network of loving, eccentric friends and family infuses the tale with a gently comic note that perfectly balances the darker dramas of the romance."
— *Publishers Weekly*

"A tender love story about two people who, when they find something special, will go to any length to keep it."
— Booklist

"Honest, witty... absolutely unforgettable."
— Rendezvous

"A classic adult fairy tale."
— *Affaire de Coeur*

"Dialogue flows easily and characters spring quickly to life."
— *Rocky Mountain News*

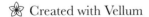

Chapter 1

CHLOE

Sugar Maple, Vermont – the day before the bridal shower

DO YOU HAVE A BIG FAMILY?

You know the kind I mean: loud and loving and always there for you when times get tough.

I have spent most of my life wishing for aunts and uncles, brothers and sisters, cousins, nieces and nephews. What can I say? I wanted hand-me-downs from my older sister, noogies from my big brother, and little siblings who would look up to me, even when I didn't deserve it. But, most of all, I wished for a mother and father. I was orphaned at six when both of my parents died in a terrible car crash and from that moment on, it seemed like I was searching for someone to call my own.

Don't get me wrong. I was never alone. After my parents' deaths, I was taken in by Sorcha, a wise and loving crone, who postponed piercing the veil to raise me to adult-hood and into my magick.

I forgot to tell you about the magick, didn't I? I'm Chloe Hobbs, the half-human, half-magick owner of Sticks & Strings, the most popular yarn shop in New England . . . and one day Planet Earth, if business keeps growing the way it has been. I'm also the *de facto* mayor of Sugar Maple, a tiny blip on the Vermont map, where centuries ago other magick types had found refuge during the Salem witch trials. Thanks to a powerful charm invoked by my ancestor Aerynn, Sugar Maple has been hiding in plain sight here in the world of humans for as long as anyone could remember and right now it's up to me to keep that chain unbroken.

Sorcha quickly discovered that raising a future sorceress really did take a village and the inhabitants of Sugar Maple rose to the challenge. An entire village of magickal beings, Fae and witch and shifter and were-family and troll and vampire, who had been hiding in plain sight for centuries.

They were right there by my side as I grew up, cheering me on. In retrospect, I guess it wasn't entirely out of the goodness of their hearts. The future of our town rested on my half-human, half-sorceress-in-training shoulders and the sooner I claimed the birthright established by Aerynn, my ancestor and the founder of Sugar Maple, the better off we'd all be.

The years passed and I grew older and taller and more human by the minute. It seemed I had about as much sorcery in me as a Magic 8 Ball. The only thing I had inherited from Aerynn and her descendants was a talent for knitting and bad luck with men.

And then, not too long before my thirtieth birthday, I fell

in love with Luke MacKenzie. My magick blossomed. I gave birth to our very magickal baby girl, Laria.

And I said yes.

I never thought I would say yes to anyone, mostly because I never really believed anyone would ask. I'm not exactly great marriage material. A human bloodline isn't very appealing to my magick friends. And, let's get real here, most humans would run screaming from my family tree.

Unless you were lucky enough to find the one human in a million strong enough to take a giant step into the unknown, all in the name of love.

I guess it's no surprise if I tell you that Luke is definitely that one human in a million strong enough to embrace the fact that the woman he loved was the daughter of a sorceress, descendant of a long line of sorceresses, and whose destiny was tied forever to a tiny magickal town hiding in plain sight in northern Vermont.

This is my home. This is my destiny. This was where I was born and from where one day, long after Luke was gone, I will pierce the veil. I will never retire to Florida or buy a cottage in Cornwall or even move to Boston to be closer to Luke's family. I'll be right here in Sugar Maple.

There will be no sons for Luke to play catch with. No more daughters either, for that matter. Descendants of Aerynn bear one child and that child was always a female who would carry our line forward toward the next millennium.

Kind of takes the fun out of family planning, doesn't it?

Then again, when it comes to family planning, the MacKenzie clan takes it to a whole new level.

Now that Luke and I are engaged and have set a wedding date, his large and loud and basically wonderful family has taken over our lives and I am quickly learning how to navigate within that strange new world.

You've heard about bridezillas, those scary women who would sell their first-born for a Vera Wang hand-embroidered original. Well, let me introduce you to Momzilla, aka my future mother-in-law Bunny MacKenzie.

Don't get me wrong. I love this woman. Despite the fact that 1) I am not going to take the family name after Luke and I wed or 2) move closer to the family, Bunny has been my number one champion. She loves Laria to distraction, showers me with affection and good advice (even when I don't ask for it or need it), and she is a first-class knitter who singlehandedly could keep Sticks & Strings in business for the next decade.

She is also the nosiest woman I've ever met.

Seriously.

Not nasty nosy. Plain, old garden-variety nosy. The kind of nosy you probably wouldn't even notice if you didn't have something to hide.

Secrets? We have a million of them and as the descendant of Aerynn it's up to me to make sure they stay that way.

Which hasn't exactly been easy now that I was part of a loud, loving family of humans.

Falling in love with Luke brought my powers to life but learning how to use those powers has been more problematic. I've made a few mistakes along the way—some worse than others—but I liked to think I was keeping one step ahead of our baby daughter Laria who is showing signs of being blessed in the magick department.

"I have a surprise for you," Bunny said, as she helped me shelve a new shipment of cashmere from Jade Sapphire.

"Besides the surprise bridal shower tomorrow?" I asked.

She tossed a skein of lace-weight at me and laughed. "I need to have a word with that son of mine. He inherited my big mouth."

"Don't blame Luke, Bunny," I said, praying she wouldn't turn around and see her eight-month-old granddaughter levitating a foot above her makeshift crib. "I badgered him."

"He grew up with siblings. He should know how to handle badgering by now."

I dusted off the skein of lace-weight and put it back on the pile. "So what's the surprise?"

Her hazel eyes sparkled with excitement. "You know I've been working on a MacKenzie family tree for a few years now."

I nodded and struggled to keep my expression neutral. The mention of family trees always made me break out in a cold sweat. "Last I heard, you found a link to the Revolutionary War on Jack's side."

"Even better! I added branches for you and for Laria. You are now officially MacKenzies." She paused for a second then winked at me. "No matter what name you go under."

My stomach twisted into a double sailor's knot. The human side of me was thrilled to finally be part of a big, loud, loving family. The magick side, however, was starting to freak out.

"Tiny branches, I hope. I don't have any blood relations." The only things I knew about my human father was his name (Ted Aubry), that he was born in Maine, and the fact that he had been studying medicine before he fell under my mother Guinevere's spell.

Were his parents still alive? Did he have siblings?

Cousins? Aunts or uncles? I hadn't a clue and, to be honest, I never asked. Sorcha had told me that he had turned away from his human family when he married Guinevere and the fact that nobody had ever showed up in Sugar Maple, with questions about his death or his baby daughter, spoke volumes. Still, I wasn't comfortable with the idea of Bunny poking around or of the questions she might ask about him.

And, let's get real, not even Ancestry.com could trace my magickal lineage. Only the Book of Spells could do that and so far it was holding its secrets close.

"I don't have much information yet," Bunny went on, mercifully unaware of my growing panic, "but don't worry. I've had a lot of practice tracking down family." Her eyes twinkled with amusement. "Nobody's safe from me!"

"'NOBODY'S SAFE FROM ME!'" I repeated to Luke a few hours later as we ate mac and cheese at the kitchen counter.

"Her exact words?" he asked, forking up a mound of cheesy goodness.

"Verbatim." I dropped my fork onto the plate. "This is a nightmare!"

Luke was quiet for a moment. "It's not like she's going to find out your mother was a sorceress."

Luke is a former Boston homicide detective, now Sugar Maple chief of police. He tends to think like a cop, which means he can be annoyingly logical.

"Exactly," I said, barely swallowing down a sigh of exasperation. "She's not going to find *anything*." I stabbed a forkful of gooey elbow macaroni for emphasis. "Zip. Nada. Not one single leaf or branch on my mother's family tree."

"Genealogy is a lot of work," he reasoned to my growing annoyance. "My mother's run into blank slates before. It's part of the process. It will seem normal to her."

"I'm nothing *but* blank slates!" I was starting to sound a little crazy but I couldn't help it. "The only place she'll find my mother is on my parents' marriage license. Other than that, I might as well have been dropped here from Mars." And that was assuming they'd actually had a license.

"Venus," he said, a grin playing at the corners of his mouth. "Definitely Venus."

"You're not funny," I snapped, even though he kind of was. "I knew blending our families wouldn't be easy, but I wasn't expecting Bunny to start climbing my family tree."

"My mother can be intense," he said.

"I'm beginning to understand why Meghan moved away from Boston."

Meghan was Luke's youngest sister and his favorite. She had a history of falling for the wrong guy, which is a nice way of saying she had a major thing for bad boys that led her into a potentially fatal relationship with a gorgeous Fae.

"Let's just take it one crisis at a time," Luke said.

I chuckled and burrowed my nose into his armpit. "I'll be a lot happier when all of this wedding business is over and we can get back to normal." Assuming I could remember what used to pass for normal.

"MacKenzie overdose?"

"You know I love your family," I said carefully. "It's just that Sugar Maple wasn't built to accommodate free-ranging humans." We liked our mortals well enough from nine-to-five when they were spending their hard-earned money in our shops and restaurants, but once the sun went down we were a whole lot more comfortable without them.

Truth was, lately something had felt off to me. I hadn't mentioned it to anyone, mostly because I couldn't explain it to myself, much less anyone else, but the sense that there was a disturbance in Sugar Maple's force field was becoming harder to ignore.

Then again, so were the MacKenzies, who were definitely enough to cause a disturbance in anyone's force field, magick or not.

"We'll get through this," he said. "Tomorrow's the shower and in two weeks the wedding will be a memory."

"I can't wait," I murmured, my words muffled. "But I'm not all that sure your mother will go back home. She asked if she could keep a change of clothes and a toothbrush here." Just saying the words made my blood run cold.

"She'll go," Luke said. "Dad wants to take that cruise they've been talking about for years."

"An around-the-world cruise?" I sounded more hopeful than I should have.

"Bahamas," Luke said, chuckling. "Six days, seven nights."

"Right now that sounds like heaven."

"We could elope," he said. "Ditch everyone and fly to Vegas."

"One small problem," I reminded him. "My paperwork is pretty much non-existent. You need proof you exist before you can get a marriage license." Here in Sugar Maple that wasn't a problem, but the rest of the world might find it a bit strange.

"Have the Book of Spells whip something up for you."

I hated to admit it, but that wasn't a bad idea. "When it comes to the Book, I'm still barely literate."

"You nailed the emergency section right out of the

gate," he reminded me, "and managed to save the town from Isadora and Dane."

"I did, didn't I?" I could hear the pride in my voice. A charm pulled from the Book of Spells might be a Def Con option, but I was hoping to find a way that couldn't backfire on Bunny or Meghan or any other human MacKenzie. Whatever it was, I'd better find it soon since the wedding was in two weeks.

"'Tis as I said 'twould be," a familiar nails-on-the-blackboard voice rang out from the doorway. "Consort with humans and trouble follows."

Elspeth, our combination nanny/surrogate grandmother/Greek chorus, floated toward us with Laria in her arms.

Luke locked eyes with his baby girl and Laria broke free from the yellow-haired troll and surfed the air straight into her Daddy's arms.

"There be exceptions," Elspeth said, her fierce expression softening. "Not many, but a few."

Who would have thought Elspeth would become Luke's fiercest supporter in Sugar Maple? I don't think anyone saw that coming. Luke still didn't quite believe it but there was no denying the affection Elspeth felt toward the father of the next generation of Aerynn and Samuel's descendants. She was even willing to overlook the fact that he didn't have a drop of magick in him.

Both Elspeth and I had offered him the chance to acquire some but to his credit Luke had declined. While I loved the fact that he was one hundred percent Homo sapiens, I have to admit there was a part of me that wished he would accept at least a smattering of magick if only to be able to protect himself from—well, from the unknown. If the last two years had taught us anything, it had taught us that danger was everywhere. Not even a powerful centuries-old protective charm had been able to save Sugar Maple from chaos and it was in our best interests to be prepared.

Unfortunately, nothing could have prepared us for what the fates had in store.

Chapter 2

CHLOE

The day of the bridal shower

"HOW MANY RELATIVES does your guy have anyway?" Janice Meany, my BFF and the owner of Cut & Curl, whispered in my ear. "The last time I saw this many humans in one place, you were running a BOGO sale on Wollmeise sock yarn."

Janice was right. My little cottage was bursting at the seams with guests, many of whom were related to Luke. I couldn't believe such a small space could hold so many people. (And that didn't include the ones visiting from other planes of existence.) They had spilled out into both the front and back yards and the decibel level had sent my house cats fleeing to safety under the bed.

"They're a fertile group," I remarked with a shake of my head. "Gotta give them that."

"And nosy." Lynette, co-owner of the Sugar Maple Arts Playhouse and my other BFF, popped up next to us. She was a shifter who usually manifested as a bright yellow canary and sometimes forgot to complete the transition.

"Don't mind me," I said, patting her down. "I'm checking for feathers."

"You won't find any," she said, shooting me a look. "I swore off shifting until the wedding."

"Lynette's right about them being nosy," Janice said, her voice low. "Bunny asked me if I had any photos of your parents."

"Why would she do that?" I asked, my anxiety level ratcheting up another notch. If there were any photos, I would have made a zillion copies and papered my walls with them.

"Because she's nosy," Lynette said. "I think it's a human thing."

"Like we're not nosy?" I shot back. "I caught Midge rummaging through my desk a few minutes ago." Midge Stallworth and her husband George were vampires who ran the infrequently used funeral home in town. "She said she was looking for a tissue but –"

"Did you hear yourself?" Janice said with a gleeful laugh. "You said, 'we're not nosy.'"

"I think that's the first time you didn't automatically identify as one of them," Lynette said.

I wasn't exactly sure how I felt about that. Being human had been my entire identity for the first thirty years of my life. No matter how powerful my magick grew, I would never turn my back on my father's side.

"You know I appreciate everything you did to make this

shower happen," I said to Janice and Lynette, "but I don't think I'll breathe easy until after the wedding."

"We couldn't manage it alone," Janice, honest to a fault, said. "We had to beg Renate for help. There was no way we could explain why an empty inn had no vacancies." No vacancies for humans, that is.

We'd gotten away with it once when Laria was christened, but I don't think we could have bluffed our way through it a second time.

The Sugar Maple Inn was run by the Weavers, a family of Fae, who when they weren't taking human form to deal with the occasional mortal guest, lived happily under the windowsills of the big house. The Inn was a centuries-old fixture in town, a well-known stopping place along the Spirit Trail. It boasted sixteen beautifully furnished rooms, all of which were usually occupied by time travelers in need of a break in their travels, and spirits looking for a place to meet in peace and safety.

Spirits wander at night. (Trust me on that one.) All we needed was for one of the MacKenzie clan to wake up with a lusty pirate asleep on the next pillow.

When Luke's ex-wife spent one very eventful night at the Inn a few years ago, I had learned first-hand why a "No Occupancy" sign was always on when humans were afoot.

In a surprisingly generous move, the Weavers had promised the Inn would be closed to the usual magick visitors until after the wedding and would be available only to the MacKenzie clan. She had issued a global blueflame announcement to that effect that had stirred up a bit of a buzz along the Spirit Trail.

"You must have called in quite a few favors to get her to do that," I said, eyeing my friends with a hint of suspicion.

"Renate isn't about to alienate her regulars unless there's something in it for her."

"I don't mean to go all Pollyanna on you, but I think she's trying to be nice," Lynette said.

"I agree," Janice, our resident cynic, chimed in. "I think she still feels guilty for siding with the opposition over moving Sugar Maple into the mist before Laria was born."

That had been a terrible time for all of us. The ancient bonds between us had been stretched to the breaking point as warring Fae factions tried to tear us apart over my half-human nature.

"I owe you one," I said, suppressing a shiver. "I'm running out of ways to keep Luke's family from figuring us out."

"A good sleeping spell might help," Lynette offered. "Wake 'em up with a goody bag and a thanks-for-coming when it's over."

Tempting but not my speed.

At least, not yet.

Everywhere you looked, MacKenzies and magicks mingled over the pinwheel sandwiches and cocktail shrimp. The humans were well-represented by Luke's family but Sugar Maple was holding its own. Lilith, our town librarian, represented the Norwegian trolls, while Midge Stallworth and Verna Griggs stood up for vampires and were-folk. Even though I didn't see her, I knew Elspeth was somewhere in the cottage. (That old waffle smell was unmistakable.) Shifters, witches, Fae from every division, they had all showed up for the occasion.

So far everyone was on her best behavior, but it was early. There was still a lot of resistance from some quarters over my commitment to a full-blood human but with Laria's birth, I sensed a turn-around might be in motion. I had secured a new generation of Hobbs to lead Sugar Maple and although that new generation had even more human blood than I, at only eight months of age her magick was already a wonder to behold.

But I was on shaky ground and I knew it. Marrying Luke and welcoming his family into our lives went against centuries of fear and distrust. I could only hope that the excitement would die down after our wedding, and life in Sugar Maple would go back to what we considered normal.

"Caution," Janice murmured. "Human approaching."

I managed not to point out the obvious.

Meghan, a glass of punch in her right hand, joined us. "Run!" she said to me, her eyes twinkling much the way Luke's did when he was amused. "There's still time."

I gestured toward the baby who was being passed from doting MacKenzie to doting MacKenzie like a cooing foot-ball. "Too late. I'm in it for life."

Janice and Lynette drifted away, leaving me alone with my soon-to-be sister-in-law.

"I'm just joking," she said, taking a sip of punch. "But you are looking a little overwhelmed."

I didn't deny it. "Overwhelmed but grateful. I always wanted to be part of a big family."

"And I always wanted to be an only child."

"Another joke?" I asked.

She shook her head but didn't elaborate and I didn't push.

Currently she was both single and celibate and deter-mined to stay that way while she did the work necessary to resume the pre-law studies she had abandoned a few years ago in pursuit of her own happily-ever-after love story. I wasn't convinced law was the right path for her, but she seemed happy so I kept my opinion to myself.

"I would have eloped," Meghan said as we watched Bunny place the baby on one of the sofas near the empty fireplace.

"Your brother suggested that."

"He's not big on these ginormous family gatherings."

"So I've noticed."

Meghan opened her mouth to say something then stopped. A startled look crossed her face. "Did you feel that?"

I started to say no when a weird rumbling sensation erupted underfoot.

"Not to worry," I said. "It's probably the furnace giving up the ghost." (A little Sugar Maple humor that only I appreciated.)

"The furnace in August? It feels more like a mini-earthquake."

"We don't do earthquakes in Vermont."

The last time the earth moved like this, the Fae had been staging a takeover attempt. Not exactly a piece of information I wanted to share.

I glanced around the room. Clearly the rum punch Elspeth had made was doing its job. Nobody else seemed to notice that the room was vibrating.

"I was in California last year for a 3.2," Meghan continued, "and it felt an awful lot like this."

I was about to spout some nonsense about the mountains and the valleys when the shaking intensified and grabbed everyone's attention. Including mine.

"Stand in the doorways, people," Luke's Aunt Peggy

called out in her retired drill sergeant voice. "You'll be safer there."

Unfortunately there were more people than available doorways in my small cottage.

Before I could draw my next breath, the house seemed to do a tap dance on its foundation and a squadron of MacKenzies (and more than a few Sugar Maples) made a run for the front door.

"The baby!" Meghan said, her tone frantic with worry. "Where is she?"

I was trying not to freak out. "Your mom has her." A grandmother who was a retired nurse. I told myself Laria couldn't be safer.

Skeins and hanks and balls of yarn tumbled from their hiding places in an explosion of color. The attic stairs dropped down without warning in an avalanche of cardboard boxes and old Tupperware containers. Cups and glasses and plates rattled. Silverware slid from the tabletops and clattered to the floor. My spinning wheel tilted crazily and skated across the room. Unfortunately, all the magazines, unread mail, baby toys, and assorted articles of clothing I'd stuffed into any available space also spilled out into view.

So now they knew Luke wasn't marrying Martha Stewart.

I could live with that.

Laria was wide-eyed and gurgling happily on the sofa, oblivious to what was going on around her. Clearly, earthquakes were a good thing in her world. She seemed positively delighted by the goings-on. Poor Bunny had been knocked on her butt a few feet away and was scrambling to regain her footing. The baby saw me and started squirming in my direction, all smiles and outstretched chubby arms, as I raced toward her across the shifting floor. The cottage lurched east, then west, and just before I reached her, Laria rose up to the ceiling then floated into my waiting arms, but not before a few graceful mid-air acrobatic loops I prayed nobody noticed.

I grabbed my giggling daughter and glanced around. Janice winked at me from across the room as Meghan, her back to me, helped Bunny to her feet. Talk about dodging a bullet.

"Are you okay?" I asked calmly, as if this sort of thing happened every day in Sugar Maple.

"The baby," Bunny said, brushing dust from the back of her summer dress. "I shouldn't have left her alone."

"No harm done," I said easily, trying not to notice the knot of magicks and humans untangling themselves near the back door. Midge Stallworth was practically nuzzling Luke's sister-in-law Tiffany. Put a vampire close to the warmth of living human flesh and trouble usually follows, no matter how evolved said vampire claimed to be.

Definitely too close for comfort in my book.

I turned back to Bunny who was still terribly upset.

"I stepped away for a second to get one of those throw pillows to make a nest for the baby and then—" She waved her hands in the air in a gesture of bewilderment. "An earthquake?!"

"Could be," Luke's Aunt Peggy joined us. "I read that there's a volcano or something developing under Vermont and part of New Hampshire. A huge upswell of heat that geologists have their eyes on."

"I read that article too," I chimed in, "but it will take millions of years for it to amount to anything."

Good going, Chloe. I had just stomped all over the perfect explanation. When will I learn to keep my big mouth shut?

"I'm surprised Luke didn't come running home to see if you're okay," Midge Stallworth snarked as she rolled by, toting two trays of finger sandwiches aloft.

"Or call," Renate Weaver, owner of the Sugar Maple Inn, added as she saved a platter of butter cookies from ruin. "You think he'd call."

My mind shot off in a thousand different directions, sparking visions of Luke trapped under a pile of rubble.

I couldn't blueflame him. My landline was defunct. And I never could find my cellphone when I needed it.

Meghan pulled an iPhone from the back pocket of her skinny jeans, pressed a few buttons, and handed it to me. "It's ringing," she said.

Luke had barely said hello when I pounced. "Are you okay? Did the quake do much damage?"

There was a long pause and then he said, "How much punch have you had anyway?"

My intestines knotted themselves into macramé. "You didn't feel the earthquake?"

"Earthquake? Screw the punch," Luke said. "Have you been hitting the Johnny Walker Black?"

I took that as a no.

"Stay put," he said. "I'll swing by in the squad car and see what's going on."

I handed the phone to Meghan who was looking at me with intense curiosity.

"So what did he say?"

"He's fine."

"Any damage?"

"None to speak of." I took a deep breath. "It seems like the quake was pretty localized."

Like right under my cottage?

This had Fae stink all over it.

"He's only a few blocks away. Wouldn't you think he'd feel something?"

"Call and ask him yourself," I snapped. "I'm not a geologist."

Meghan's cheeks turned bright red and instantly I was ashamed of myself.

"I'm sorry," I said. "I shouldn't have snapped at you like that. I don't know what's going on and that bothers me."

"Understandable," she said. "It was pretty scary."

Next to us, Verna Griggs, matriarch of an esteemed were-family, gave a snort of laughter. "Hurricanes are scary. Blizzards are scary. This was nothing more than a cheap amusement park ride."

Meghan rolled her eyes. We both knew that only seconds ago, Verna had been clutching her beads. "I'm going to sweep up the broken glass and china," she said and headed toward the kitchen for a broom.

"Good idea," her mother seconded. "If we all pitch in, we can have everything put back in two shakes of a lamb's tail."

"No!" I said. "Everyone, stop what you're doing! This is a party. I'll take care of this later." I mean, what was the point to keeping a battery of house sprites on retainer if you didn't use them?

"This is your day," Bunny said, giving Laria's tiny foot a grandmotherly kiss. "We'll put everything to rights and get this party back on track."

And the funny thing is, I actually believed her. The

MacKenzie women in action were a sight to behold. I'm not sure a battalion of sprites could do better. Peggy and Bunny assessed the damage, divided the work, and then set the rest of the family to getting it done in record time. You know those commercials where a crew of specialists swoop down on a house and make the damage from fires and floods disappear? That was exactly what those wonderful women did.

Janice motioned for me to join her in the kitchen.

"It was Forbes," she said in a whisper. The Mountain Giant had decided to join the party and had dragged a forty-foot spruce with a root ball the size of a Ford Explorer down from his lair as a wedding present.

"And that caused an earthquake?" It didn't make sense.

"It does if you drop it." Janice looked like she was stifling a laugh. "I told him the shower was for girls only and he couldn't join us."

"Were his feelings hurt?" Forbes was a very high-strung giant.

"I promised him three extra pieces of wedding cake."

"What about the tree?"

"House sprites," she said. "It took twenty of them, but the tree is back where it started."

And that was only the beginning.

Chapter 3

CHLOE

"THIS MUST HAVE FALLEN from the attic," Bunny said as she pulled a dented pale yellow shoebox out from under one of the end tables. "Look! It has your name on it."

CHLOE was clumsily printed in green crayon across the lid. A red plaid ribbon held the box closed. It smelled vaguely of cinnamon and spice and the indefinable scent that would always remind me of my mother.

"Honey, are you okay?" Bunny leaned close. "You look like you've seen a ghost."

"I have," I whispered. Once upon a time, that shoebox had held my most beloved treasures. I used to take it with me wherever I went.

"Give me the baby," she said, "and you take the box."

We did a quick swap. My hands were shaking so hard I'm surprised she didn't rush me to a hospital.

I wanted to run to the bedroom I shared with Luke and spill the contents of the box across the bed but I was too impatient. Instead I sat down on the sofa, fumbled with the ribbon, then tossed the lid to the floor by my feet. Meghan had joined us but she barely registered on my radar.

"Oscar!" I sounded like the six-year-old I had once been. The stuffed pink frog stared up at me as memories flooded in. Oscar had been my boon companion for as far back as I could remember. The small, scruffy toy had been with me on that terrible night—

I shook my head. Only good memories today.

I was aware of Bunny's sharp eyes taking in every last detail but for once I didn't care. She was sitting at the other end of the couch with the baby on her lap.

"I'll bet he was your best friend," she said, jiggling a squirmy Laria. "All of my kids had a friend like your Oscar."

"You should ask Luke about his dinosaur," Meghan said with a wicked grin. "Your wedding night would be a great time."

I started to laugh.

Meghan joined in. "And make sure to tell him who to thank."

"My diary," I whispered as I picked up the tiny locked volume. "My father taught me how to read and write when I was four."

The two women exchanged glances.

"He sounds like he was a good dad," Bunny said carefully.

I nodded, my heart bursting with remembered joy and fresh sorrow. "He was."

I pulled out a wrinkled white handkerchief, three knitted

swatches in various shades of purple, one mahogany knitting needle, a set of car keys on a cheap fob, and a man's argyle sock in progress.

"Maybe there are some photos in there," Meghan said. "I'd love to see a picture of your parents."

"So would I," I said softly. "But there aren't any." Not anywhere.

"Not even a wedding photo," Meghan went on, "or maybe something from your christening. You--"

Bunny gave her daughter a kick in the shin.

"What?" Meghan protested. "Like you don't wonder the same thing, Ma?"

"Regret," Bunny corrected her, "not wonder." She met my eyes. "Of course we'd love to see a picture of the people who brought you into the world, but I know you don't have any."

Their open curiosity didn't matter to me. I was swept back to a time when I had been happy, safe and secure with two parents who loved me. A time I thought would never end.

It felt like someone else's life. Someone else's dream.

But it was mine and it was coming at me like a freight train.

I AM BUCKLED into the back seat of the car, snuggled beneath a mountain of blankets, and surrounded by some of my favorite things. My diary. My Sleeping Beauty coloring book and a fat box of crayons.

And Oscar.

Oscar is my favorite. I refuse to go anywhere without the stuffed frog. He has been with me as long as I can remember which, consid-ering the fact that I am barely six years old, isn't that long.

Music spills from the radio. It's been a long day and I am dozing off in the warm car.

Snow falls beyond the windows, a wintry landscape rolling by my sleepy eyes.

In the front seat, my parents talk softly as my father guides the car safely along the icy road. Bits and pieces of their conversation float past me, a jumble of words I don't really understand and for many years won't remember.

"I hope we did the right thing, Guin." My father's voice is warm, like a hug after a nightmare.

My mother is quiet and I wonder if she fell asleep but then she speaks. To me her voice sounds like music. "She'll be protected all her life," I hear her say. "Given our situation, that's no small thing."

"It's like living in some strange fairy tale written hundreds of years ago," my father says, his voice snapping like branches breaking in a storm. "We could move away. Start fresh somewhere normal—"

"Sugar Maple is our home," my mother says. I see her hand reach out and stroke my father's dark hair. "One day Chloe will be the heart and soul of it."

The silence stretched.

"You're not listening to me, Teddy. Nothing like this has happened before in our history."

"Three hundred years and nobody else fell in love with a mortal?"

"Friendships were almost impossible between magicks and mortals until fairly recently. A marriage . . . a child —" She paused for what seemed like forever. "They're terrified this will somehow make it possible for the humans to destroy us."

"I'm human and they've accepted me."

"To a degree. The collective memory is strong. We're only a heart-beat away from the days of cruelty and persecution."

"And you think our decision will keep Chloe safe if things go bad?"

"As soon as we cross the Sugar Maple town line, the Fae will know and the news will spread like a blessing."

"And this decision will keep her safe?"

As always, my mother's touch soothes my father in ways I sense but don't understand.

"Trust me, Teddy." Her voice is low and melodic. *"If we change our minds, we can break the bonds up until her twenty-first birthday."*

"There's time," he says at last, glancing toward my mother. *"Plenty of time."*

EXCEPT THERE WASN'T.

~

"OH, LOOK!" Meghan's voice brought me back into the moment. "Laria wants to check out the shoebox."

The baby wiggled her way out of her grandmother's grasp and was stretching her chubby arms toward the box on my lap.

"Good grief," Bunny said. "She wants that scruffy little pink frog."

"No, sweetie." I thrust poor Oscar behind my back. "I think he might be toxic."

"It's the light," Lilith, our town librarian/historian, pointed out as she scurried past with a broom and dustpan. "It's captured her attention."

We all looked at each other.

"What light?" I asked.

"She knows," Lilith said, laughing, as Laria thrust a baby fist into the shoebox and pulled out a ring.

The ring was the deep burnished color of Welsh gold, same as the ring that I had inherited from my mother, but the resemblance ended there. My ring was an unadorned circle of gold. This ring was all bumps and angles and deep scratches along the surface.

And it glowed.

"It seems like it's lit from within," Meghan said.

"It's the sun." I pointed toward the window. "See how it's hitting the ring just right?"

"The ring itself is glowing, honey," Bunny said. "Since when does gold glow like that?"

"Aftershocks." Janice swooped in on us. "It's all an optical illusion." She went on about refraction and angles and degree of sunlight until our eyes started to cross.

"I thought you did hair," Meghan said. "You sound like a scientist."

"Janice went to Harvard," I said. (As if that explained her string of malarkey.)

Bunny and Peggy exchanged looks that Janice pretended not to see.

Laria, however, didn't much care why the pretty ring was lit up like a glowstick.

She just wanted to eat it.

"Oh, no you don't!" I began to gently pry those chubby fingers away from the ring. "We don't eat jewelry in this house."

Her grip tightened.

The MacKenzie women zeroed in.

"Laria," I said in my best mommy-means-business voice. I could feel my cheeks burning. "Give that to me."

Superbaby gave a tug worthy of a Marvel Comics hero

and I almost fell off the sofa. I played it for comedy value but I was the only one not laughing.

Please don't, Laria! This isn't the time to parade your magick in front of your Daddy's family.

"Give a little tug," Bunny advised. "You won't hurt her."

I nodded and tugged, but to no avail. I didn't tell Bunny that I was more concerned that Laria might accidentally dislocate my shoulder. Her magick was both powerful and uncontrolled, while mine was still a work in progress.

Lynette, who had been watching from the far side of the room, did one of her patented canary whistles. Laria's grip lessened.

"That's it!" I said. "Lynette, keep distracting her."

Lynette's whistles grew louder and more intricate and the baby clearly loved them. She pursed her lips and emitted a clear, high sound that was probably heard in Montpelier.

"Holy crap!" Luke's sister-in-law Tiffany shouted out from the front porch. "Is somebody hailing a cab on Saturn?"

I didn't know where this was going, but I knew it wasn't good.

Who would have expected Renate Weaver to come to the rescue again?

"Step aside," she said with her usual degree of Fae self-confidence. "Let me show you how it's done in Sugar Maple."

She bent down until she was on eye level with Laria. No whistles. No whispers. No tricks. She leveled her amethyst gaze on the baby and instantly Laria's attention shifted from the ring to the woman in front of her.

While I was grateful for the help, I wondered what exactly my frenemy Renate was conveying to my daughter.

She had been a vocal part of the uprising that had nearly resulted in Sugar Maple leaving the human realm and retreating beyond the mist to one of the Fae dimensions. There had been a time when I considered Renate and the other Weavers as friends, good friends, but the trust had been broken and I wasn't sure it would ever come back.

Laria's grip relaxed again and I took the ring from her.

"Thanks, Renate," I said, hoping to break the almost palpable connection growing between her and my daughter. "I don't know exactly what you did, but it worked."

"Practice," Renate said with a guileless smile. "Four children, eight grandchildren. You learn."

"Seven and fifteen," Bunny said with an equally guileless smile. "I have a few tricks up my sleeve, too."

I could hear Janice and Lynette stifling their snickers from across the room.

My future mother-in-law was good, but when it came to tricks, never bet against a Fae.

"It's huge," Meghan observed of the ring. "You need man hands to wear a ring like that."

"Maybe it was your father's," Bunny said. "Wouldn't that be wonderful?" She looked closer. "Is that an inscription?"

"I don't know." I pointed to the Welsh gold circlet that I never removed. "This one was my mother's." And her mother's before her, all the way back to Aerynn and the beginning of our line. "I've never seen this other one before."

"But it was in your toy box."

I took a deep breath, held it a moment, then exhaled slowly. "Those were the things I had with me when my parents died."

Looking for a way to change the conversation? Death is a pretty good place to start.

"Oh, honey…" Bunny placed a hand on my shoulder and gave it a gentle squeeze. "I had no idea."

"Neither did I," I said. Not until a second ago.

The memory cut through to the center of my heart. I could see myself shivering in the gleaming white hospital corridor, waiting for Sorcha, my new surrogate mother, to sign the papers and take me away from that terrible place. I wanted to be back in the warm car with my mommy and daddy, safe and secure, the way every six-year-old child should be, but that life was over.

I recalled watching, frozen in place, as a nurse handed Sorcha a shoebox filled with all that remained of everything I had known.

That was the last time I'd seen the shoebox until today.

I could hear them talking all around me as they tried to determine the ring's provenance, as if *Antiques Roadshow* had come to life in northern Vermont.

The ring was gold, I could see that clearly, and it was definitely antique. It was also heavy and large. Did my father wear rings? I didn't think so. He had worked as a carpenter. A ring like this would be an encumbrance. I also couldn't imagine it on my mother's slender hand or my then-childish one.

As was the case with so many things about those years, I would never know.

However, there was little doubt that it held magick within its depths. That glowing light had nothing to do with refraction or any of the mumbo jumbo Janice had spouted, and I was grateful that either she or Lynette had cast a quick spell over the ring in an attempt to cloak its glow.

But even without the glowing light to capture her attention, Laria was still transfixed. She made another grab for it but I slipped it onto the index finger of my right hand. It was huge on me and I curled my fingers into a loose fist to keep it from falling off.

I needn't have bothered.

The ring started to blink, then seemed to encircle my finger with peace and promise, shrinking to fit before I realized what was happening. It didn't feel like metal at all but a warm, living entity that was meant to be part of me.

It felt a lot like destiny.

Suddenly I knew this wasn't going to end well.

Chapter 4

GAVAN

Beyond the mist

THEIR TIME WAS RUNNING OUT.

It had long been obvious to Gavan that their world was in its dying days. He only wondered how it was that so many of his clan didn't realize it too. Not even the combined magicks of Fae, witch, sorcerer or Others could stop the inexorable end. Like the rotation of planets around the suns and the birth of new stars, the end of their dimension was writ large. Soon it would be into the cosmos and there was nothing they could do to stop it.

The time had come to choose: either reunite with our sister clan in their earth sanctuary or pierce the veil for eternity.

When the summons came from Rohesia, he made haste to the mountainside. Rohesia was the mother of his mother, the most powerful overseer since the ancient splitting of the family aeons ago. They were a mixed clan of Fae, witch, troll, sorcerer, sprite, vampire, and Others. Over time they had found strength in diversity but it had not been without conflict. Rohesia was pure Fae, blessed with beauty and arrogance and a keen sense of survival.

She was waiting for him in the soaring natural cathedral-like cave that she called home. Some said she had conjured it from the collective memory of their beginning in an earth place called Wales but that might be legend and not fact. But it did evoke another time and place long gone when his kind had lived in peace with humans.

Before the murderous brutality that forced his kind to flee beyond the mist.

Those memories had been part of his education, a constant reminder to be on guard, to protect all they held dear, to remember that humans were a duplicitous species capable of genocide when threatened. The younger members of the clan had been making exploratory visits to the human dimension, returning with stories of peace and harmony between mortals and the Other. These days humans restricted their destruction to their own kind.

Rohesia, however, believed none of it.

Humans were devious, seeking to gather the magicks together in order to facilitate their destruction. Sugar Maple was a fortress that Aerynn had established to save her people from a brutal end in Salem.

Clearly, humans were not to be trusted.

He entered the cave. His eyes took a moment to adjust to the absence of light. He sensed rather than saw her presence.

"I am here at your request," he said, bowing his head in a gesture of respect.

She manifested with the practiced ease of one at the height of her powers. Only the faint shimmer of carnelian glitter revealed the effort it took.

The pleasantries were brief and she swiftly launched into the reason for the summons.

"Not long before the birth of your mother, the light flashes first appeared. We believed they were of little concern, only the thinning of the dimension's borders. A warning, as it were, of the eventual moment when we would blink out of existence. "

He nodded. The flashes of lightning were part of the life they shared beyond the mist.

"We believed we had an abundance of time to examine our choices and make plans for our future." Her gaze softened as she met his eyes. "We were terribly wrong."

His gut twisted. He saw his future drawing into a knot he could never untangle. Suddenly he felt the weight of the ring on his finger in a way he never had before. It seemed to grow warmer as he stood there.

"We intercepted a multidimensional blueflame sent by the Fae of Aerynn's clan. Your betrothed is marrying a human in two earth weeks' time."

He maintained a blank expression against a rising tide of relief. "The betrothal is broken?"

The force of her fury shook the walls of the cave. "The betrothal went into full effect when Chloe turned twenty-one human years. Our dimensions perceive time very differently. We waited patiently for her people to contact us about a joining, but they clearly broke our trust. That is a mistake we will now rectify."

With a wave of her bejeweled hand, she activated the betrothal rings. He felt a surge of power as the ring encircled his finger in a way it never had before. It glowed as if lit from within and then began to blink slowly. *A noose,* he thought. He would be forever bound to a half-human stranger named Chloe. A half-human stranger who had pledged herself to marry another.

Rohesia was clear in her directive. He would travel to the human dimension and after taking stock of the situation, claim Chloe of Guinevere as his own.

She would not be allowed to wed the human.

He would not be allowed to seek his own mate.

Rohesia declared that their individual lives were of little consequence when compared to the imminent destruction of an entire dimension and its people.

Gavan had no choice but to make it happen.

Chapter 5

CHLOE

NOTHING like a faux earthquake to put a damper on a bridal shower. The MacKenzies couldn't wait to get the heck out of Sugar Maple and back to the Boston area before another earthquake struck, and the locals couldn't help them leave fast enough.

I owed Forbes an extra piece of wedding cake.

The shake-up had unnerved everyone, albeit for different reasons, and by five o'clock, I was back home in yoga pants and a t-shirt.

"I did the drive-by and didn't see any evidence of seismic activity in the area," Luke said as we picked at leftovers from the shower.

"I'm not surprised," I said, shaking my head. "It wasn't an earthquake; it was Forbes."

He grabbed a handful of pinwheel sandwiches and

popped them into his mouth, one right after the other. "Forbes?"

"Forbes and a forty-foot shower gift that he accidentally dropped in my backyard."

"You want to run that by me again?"

"I'm just repeating what Janice told me." I gave him the details. "A fleet of house sprites managed to whisk the tree away before anyone saw it."

"Forbes is nocturnal," Luke said. "What the hell was he doing up during daylight?"

"Coffee," I said, unable to suppress my laughter. "He ran out of decaf and downed a bucket of espresso."

He broke into a tired grin. "And you thought my mother was going to be the problem."

"Give her time," I said with a well-timed eye roll. "I have total faith in Bunny."

"I wish I could say the same thing about Renate and the staff of the Inn."

My stomach clenched. "Why? Have you heard something? Renate has been very accommodating so far." Not only was she opening the doors of the Inn to a flurry of human MacKenzies, she had issued a universal blueflame order to suspend all magick until after the wedding.

"Yeah, she's been pretty decent, but that doesn't change the fact that eight months ago, she was ready to throw you under the bus. I don't like having her in close contact with my family."

There was nothing I could say about that. Suspicion was part of being a cop. It never quite went away.

"Forbes's mini earthquake produced a few other surprises." I told him about the shoebox containing Oscar and the mementoes from my short time with my parents.

He pulled me toward him for one of those big, warm, very human hugs that I craved more than oxygen.

"This was in the shoebox too." I held up my right hand and pointed toward the enormous that swallowed up my index finger. "I can't seem to get it off."

"Cold water?"

I shook my head.

"Butter?"

"Gross, and also ineffective."

"Magick?"

"It wouldn't budge."

"And you don't know where it came from?"

"That's right, officer. It was in the shoebox with the other stuff."

He gave me the patented dead-eyed cop look and went on. "Tell me exactly what happened, step by step."

I took a deep breath. "I'm pretty sure it's not an ordinary ring."

"This is Sugar Maple," he muttered. "Why should anything be ordinary?"

I told him about Laria's fascination with the ring. "It was huge, way too big for me, but I finally slipped it onto my index finger to get it away from her. I was wondering how I would keep it from falling off when it started to blink, then began to shrink around my finger."

"Melted?"

"Sort of. It was warm, but not hot. It all happened so quickly..."

"And now it won't come off."

"Exactly."

"I don't know how these things work," he said, still in

cop mode. "Is the ring magickal or did someone or something else make it happen?"

"You're the detective."

"You're the sorceress." A quick smile broke through, "Let me take a closer look."

I scooted closer on the couch and held out my hand. He leaned forward, took my hand, then tried to spin the ring around so he could see the underside.

"Hey, Sherlock! That finger is attached to someone you love."

Cop mode had been replaced by its scary brother, Super Cop Mode.

"Sorry," he said. "I can see striations in the gold. I think they go all the way around but I need to take a closer look." He glanced around the room. "Do we have any lighted magnification I could use?"

"Please," I said with an attempted eye roll. "I'm a knitter."

I don't know about other knitters, but I scatter notions the way Gretel scattered breadcrumbs. You never know when you might need a needlesizer or a gauge ruler or, in this case, a handy-dandy lighted magnifying bar.

"Great," he said, taking a look at it. "What do you use this for?"

"Following rows on a chart," I said. "But it multitasks well with others."

I'm not sure he heard me. He was painstakingly examining every millimeter of accessible ring.

"These aren't scratches," he said, looking up for a moment. "They're designs etched into the --" He stopped, his eye apparently caught by something new. "I changed the angle of the light and now I see another image."

The man was meticulous in his inspection. I had seen that same attention to detail at work when he first arrived in Sugar Maple to investigate the death of Suzanne Marsden.

"You say this ring was much bigger originally?"

I nodded. "Ginormous."

"Interesting," he said. "Somehow the picture etched on the surface retained its proportions when it shrank to fit your finger."

"This is Sugar Maple," I reminded him. "Anything's possible."

He did one more full inspection, and then leaned back against the sofa. "I see a group of curved lines, stair-stepped in a semi-circle. A cloud surrounds a figure floating in air, flanked by two other figures that seem to be facing outward."

"All of that in such a tiny area?"

He nodded. "And there was probably more detail that was lost to time."

"Like scrimshaw."

"Same idea, different canvas." He met my eyes. "Does any of this mean anything to you?"

"I wish it did."

"Your ancestors were big on symbols. The clouds, the stair steps--none of this rings any bells?"

"Are you sure about the images?" I asked. "I didn't see anything when I looked."

"Neither did I at first. The magnifying light helped but I think there's more at work than that."

"Magick?" I asked.

"Could be."

"How old do you think it is?"

"With gold it's hard to tell. We would need an expert to

pinpoint it exactly. This could be part of local history or a message from a UFO. Who knows?"

"You're a lot of help," I said with a shaky smile. "Good thing you're a cop and not an historian."

"Speaking of historians, Lilith might be able to help us," he said. "Nobody knows more about Sugar Maple's past than she does. Maybe she can decipher the images on the ring."

I nodded. I would be there tomorrow when the library opened.

Out of nowhere, my eyes filled with tears. "I'm scared, Luke."

"You?" He looked genuinely surprised. "I've seen you battle demons."

"This is different." I took another deep breath and centered myself. "Demons I can handle. This—" I paused, then tried again. "Maybe you're right. Maybe we really should elope." Get far away from Sugar Maple until we were safely married.

"What changed between yesterday and today?"

"Finding that shoebox...this ring." The feeling that something was lurking in the shadows, ready to destroy our happiness. I was committed to Luke in every way possible, in this world and any other we might encounter. For me, this was forever. Obtaining a license and repeating some words in front of friends and relatives wouldn't change anything. The wedding ceremony was for him and for the MacKenzies and clearly it had struck a nerve somewhere in Sugar Maple and that worried me.

Something flickered behind Luke's eyes but was gone before I could process it.

"Do you want to call off the wedding? Is that what this is really about?" he asked.

"What?"

"I'm asking a question." His tone gave away nothing. "Lately I've had the feeling you're slipping away from me."

This time I couldn't control the tears. They spilled over and ran freely down my cheeks. "That will never happen. I'm yours and I'll always be yours. Nothing can change that."

"So you want to tell me what's wrong?"

"I know what it's like to grow up without parents," I said, wiping away my tears with the back of my hands. "I don't want that to happen to Laria."

"It won't," he said, holding me tight. "I promise."

"You can't know that."

"We're going to get married and grow old together," he said. "We're going to be around to watch Laria take her rightful place here in Sugar Maple."

"Things happen," I said. "People change."

"Not us."

"You might get tired of Sugar Maple. There's a whole world out there waiting for you."

"I don't give a damn about the world," he said, pulling me into his arms. "This is my home now and it always will be."

I let myself melt into his warmth, his strength, his love. For me, that was the only magick that mattered. "You sound pretty sure of yourself."

"I am," he said.

If only I believed it too.

~

I WAITED until Luke fell into a deep sleep then I slipped out of bed and moved quietly toward the front room of the cottage. It was a moonless night and the rooms were dark but that didn't matter. I had spent most of my life in this place and I knew the location of every squeaky floorboard. I peeked in on Laria and the sight of her hovering an inch above her mattress with her adorable baby bum sticking up made my heart burst with love. Although I couldn't see her, the unmistakable smell of waffles told me her guardian Elspeth was nearby.

If only there were some way to freeze these perfect moments, when everyone you loved was happy and safe, no more than a heartbeat away.

But there wasn't and that was why I needed help from the Book of Spells. I wanted to know more about the ring that had my finger in a death grip.

Legend had it that the Book was instantly accessible at any time for an ancestor of Aerynn, but I hadn't found that to be the case. With me the Book was mercurial, just as likely to ignore my pleas for help as to grant them. Janice said it was some sort of test, a way to ensure that my magick side was finally achieving dominance over my human side, and I guess that was as good an explanation as any. From the moment my magick began to appear, I'd felt like I was being tested every second of every day.

I settled myself in the chair near my favorite spinning wheel and cleared my mind of everything but the Book of Spells. In the arcane language that was so much a part of the magicks, I called upon it to manifest in that humble room.

And then I waited. I could have knitted ten rows of the

most intricate Alice Starmore pattern in the time it took to get a response.

The air shimmered. Somewhere in the distance I heard a bell ring three times then grow silent.

"We all know you're the boss," I said, starting to grow annoyed. "Why don't you give me a break and manifest?"

I needed more practice in arcane begging.

"Please share your wisdom with this student of the Arts and shine the light of knowledge upon this golden ring."

I could almost hear the Book laugh.

"Help me," I said as simply as I could. "Show me what I need to know."

I thought of the Book as a bitchy best friend who responded well to shameless flattery and occasional groveling.

Finally I felt a buzz working its way along my nerve endings and I took a deep breath. The Book had a mind of its own, a magickal multi-media experience that sometimes delivered more than you bargained on.

Or less.

Like I said, it wasn't above being passive-aggressive.

The buzz turned into a syrupy feeling of warmth that made my limbs loose and lazy. I leaned back in the chair, willing to let the Book take me wherever it wanted me to go.

The chair rocked gently back and forth and then, as I was about to doze off, the roof parted to expose the starry sky. The chair rose and before I could comprehend what was happening, we soared into the summer night.

Summer turned to fall as I sailed above the grove of maples near Snow Lake.

Fall turned to winter.

A steady snow enveloped me in a curtain of white.

I saw nothing but snow.

I heard nothing but wind.

I waited for the Book to bring everything into focus but it didn't happen.

The snow stopped.

Winter turned back into fall.

Fall retreated into summer.

I blinked and I was back in my cottage, more confused than ever.

Chapter 6

CHLOE

AS PROMISED, I was waiting at the library door the next morning when Lilith arrived.

"I need you to take a look at the ring," I said, as I followed her inside. "We found an etching or an inscription or something and Luke thought you might be able to decipher it for us."

"I can try," she said. "No guarantees."

I helped her open up, switching on lights, opening windows, boiling water for tea.

Finally we settled down in the map room where the lighting and magnification options were many and extraordinary.

"You still can't take it off?" Lilith asked as she switched on a pair of Ott Lites and aimed the beams on my hand.

"It won't budge," I said. "And it won't stop glowing. I can see it despite the spells we cast."

"I'd love to get a look inside and see if there's an inscription of any kind."

"Me, too," I said. "But I'll settle for whatever I can get."

Lilith slipped on a pair of serious-looking glasses, leaned forward, then got to work.

"Do you see anything?" I asked.

"Honey, I've barely had time to focus."

"Sorry."

A few more decades passed.

"Stop fidgeting, Chloe, please!"

I tried. I really did. But I was desperate for answers.

Finally Lilith pulled off her glasses and switched off the lights.

I knew before she said a word.

"Nothing," I said. "Right?"

"I'm afraid not."

She had seen the same symbols Luke had. "The symbols don't match up with anything I've seen associated with Sugar Maple's history."

"No connection to the talisman?"

"Not that I'm aware of."

"Can you place an age on the ring?"

"Old," she said with a rueful laugh. "Really, really old."

"Multi-millennia old?"

"I'm not sure. Definitely multi-century." She was quiet for a long moment. "This is just a guess, but I don't think the figures are random and I don't think they're decorative. I think it's a form of story-telling."

"Like the cave walls in France?"

"Exactly. This is part of a story someone wanted to pass along."

But what the story was remained a mystery.

It was still early and I was reluctant to give up so easily. Lilith had to get to work but she said I could continue going through the archive of accumulated symbols and images associated with Sugar Maple.

I had an hour until Sticks & Strings opened. Maybe luck would be on my side and point me in the right direction.

I was sick of the stupid ring. I was tired of thinking about mini-earthquakes and nosy relatives. I was done with talking about wedding dresses, wedding cakes, wedding guests. I couldn't wait for it all to be over so Luke and Laria and I could just go back to being a family.

"I'm done," I said to the empty room. The ring was going to stay where it was until after the wedding, even if I had to cover it with duct tape and a pair of garden gloves.

I put the files back in the cabinet, turned off the slide projector, and was about to hunt down Lilith to say thanks and see you later, when a bolt of lightning shot down from the right-hand corner of the ceiling and bounced off the mystery ring. A cloud of carnelian-red mist rose up from the ring, filling the room with a vaguely floral scent I couldn't identify and wasn't sure I liked.

The silence was profound yet it throbbed with energy.

The room around me no longer existed. At least not in its earthbound form. Walls disappeared. The ceiling drifted away. The floor melted at my feet. Orientation didn't matter. There was no up, no down, no compass to guide me.

There was no choice. I inhaled deeply and gave myself over to whatever was coming my way and in that instant of surrender, the Book revealed itself.

Now we were getting somewhere.

In the far distance, through a cloud of now icy-grey mist, a figure beckoned. A shape, really, tall and slender, wearing the unmistakable jeweled robes of a leader. Somehow I knew it was the legendary Rohesia. Her pull was magnetic. It drew me toward her, faster and faster through swirling red and orange mists and random bolts of lightning. But no matter how quickly I moved or how far I traveled, I couldn't bridge the gap between us.

She had the answer I was seeking. I knew it in the center of my being. If I could only manage to reach her, I would understand what was happening and be able to bend circumstances to my advantage.

I was feeling hopeful that the Book of Spells was about to open its pages wide when the mist surrounding me went from icy-grey to blood red and the deep silence was pierced by screams that seemed to come from the limits of human endurance.

The mist vanished and the horrific scene before me was illuminated with brutal clarity. This was the human realm. I registered that in my own very human nerve endings. Not the era I knew. Men garbed in tunics pulled women and children screaming from huts with thatched roofs on fire from flaming torches thrown crazily into the crowd. I didn't want to believe those ugly faces contorted with rage came from the same species of creature as half of me did, but I knew it was true.

I closed my eyes against the sight but words formed themselves deep within and forced me to bear witness.

Look, Chloe . . . look and remember!

I didn't want to look. I didn't want to remember. I knew the stories of the atrocities humans had visited on the magicks. I didn't need a reminder. I wanted to believe times had changed, that the world was a better, more inclusive place. The world wasn't quite ready to embrace the Other, but we were making progress. Maybe one day a sanctuary like Sugar Maple wouldn't be necessary.

See what is real . . . not what you wish to be real.

Evil lived. It was all around me, smothering me with the stink of flame and flesh. Soldiers dragged the terrified women and children to the center of the small town where men, chained to towering pyres of flame, were being burned alive. Swords slashed through the living, severing arms and legs, while terrified horses whinnied and dragged wagons over innocents as they tried to flee the fiery carnage.

Cries of "Devil!" and "Witch!" rose above the high-pitched screams of agony.

This was hell. This was evil incarnate, chaos taken to a level of insanity that turned humans into monsters and monsters into victims.

They were both my people. My blood. No matter who won, I would be on the losing side.

A wail rose from the center of my soul, a keening cry I couldn't control, didn't want to control.

And then I saw him.

He walked out of the flames, through the chaos, heading toward me with his powerful arms outstretched. He was both strange to me and familiar, as if he had been part of a life unknown to me. He was impervious to flame and sword. Tall and strong, he wore simple breeches and a dark cloak embroidered with Dewi, Y Ddraig Goch, David the Red Dragon of Cadwallader from Welsh mythology, which was at the heart of Sugar Maple's ancient history.

I tried to look away but I couldn't. The power he had

over me was absolute. Somehow I knew this man could change my life in ways that terrified me. He could take everything from me that mattered.

The ring on my finger began to blink. An otherworldly glow, different from what I'd grown accustomed to, emanated from it, casting light into the middle distance.

I summoned up every ounce of magick at my command, every drop of human will and strength I had and in the instant before I could see his face, the flames receded, the floor rolled back out beneath my feet, the walls slid back into place, the ceiling returned, and I was back in the library on a sunny morning in Sugar Maple, just as if nothing had happened.

∾

GAVAN

HE CURSED the Book of Spells as he inspected the charred sleeve of his garment. He had long heard of its power over all magicks but he had not believed it until now when it forced him into Chloe's dreamscape. He had barely made the transition between dimensions when he found himself thrust into yet another strange world.

She was looking for answers and the Book knew that he and Rohesia could provide them, but now was not the time.

To live and thrive in this dimension would require more of their old world magick than he had anticipated. He was young and strong but even he felt his resources exhausted by the journey. He understood why making the move between dimensions had once seemed almost impossible to Rohesia.

He retreated to the waterfall portal where he had entered this dimension to replenish his magick and reconsider his options.

~

CHLOE

Later that evening

"SO LUKE COULDN'T PRY the damn thing off either?" Janice asked me as we gathered for the weekly Knit Night at the shop.

"He suggested that we try a hacksaw, but I drew the line at bloodletting."

That got a few laughs from the usual subjects gathered around the long work table and I could feel my nerves settling back into place. As awful as it sounded, I was grateful the extended MacKenzie clan had gone back to Massachusetts and wouldn't return until the wedding. To be honest, I wouldn't have minded if they stayed away until Christmas.

I needed time to wrap a little normal around my shoulders like a lace-weight shawl and just be me.

I was working on the last inches of a crisp, summery bolero for the baby to wear to the wedding. Sharp lemon yellow, pure white, and touches of saturated cobalt blue, all in a surprisingly buttery washable linen blend. I love the natural colors of wool as much as the next knitter, but there are times when you crave color and this was one of them.

"So what are you going to do about the ring?" Lynette asked.

"I was going to ask all of you," I said. "There has to be a spell somewhere that can get this thing off my finger."

"There probably is," Lilith said, looking up from the tiny sock she was working with toothpick-sized double points, "but first we'd have to find out which spell caused the problem in the first place."

"So you think it's already under a spell, too?"

Another burst of laughter from the table.

"Oh, honey!" Lilith leaned across and patted me on the hand. "Of course it's a spell. Somebody somewhere is trying to make a little mischief with some very bad magick."

"I'm not sure if that's good news or bad news," I said.

Janice made a sound somewhere between a laugh and a snort. "The answer is simple. Luke's people have some powerful juju going for them. Their sheer mass disrupted the energies in Chloe's cottage and they're letting you know they don't like it."

"They pissed somebody off big time," Midge Stallworth squeaked. She was looking particularly rosy-skinned tonight. I tried very hard not to think about why. "My hair down-right tingled until they crossed the state line and were back in Massachusetts."

"They are Irish," Lynette said with a knowing nod. "I've never met a human of Irish descent who didn't have some connection to the other dimensions."

"That's right," Lilith agreed. "And put a few dozen of them in one highly-charged area and there are bound to be repercussions."

"I like your theory," I said, "but I'm pretty sure the MacKenzie clan is of Scottish descent."

"The name may be," Lilith said, not missing a beat, "but

their vibe is one hundred percent Irish and you know what that means."

"So what you're saying is that the MacKenzies pissed off some invisible Sugar Maple leprechauns who decided to ruin the party."

"Chloe, really." Verna Griggs, who wasn't even a knitter, shot me a look dripping with pity as she worked on a quilt top. "Everyone knows there's no such thing as leprechauns."

The laughter took a while to die down but when it did, things got serious fast.

"I don't want to worry you, Chloe, but I think Luke's mother is up to something," Lilith said as she wound a center-pull ball of indie-dyed merino. "She emailed me after lunch, asking all sorts of questions about your father."

"My father?" My stomach dropped into my feet. "What kinds of questions?"

"She asked a few questions about your mother, too, but I deflected them with our usual 'we're digitizing them for the state' excuse. But then she started on your father: where was he born, how old was he when he died, did I know anything about his people—typical genealogical questions, but she was pretty insistent."

"What did you tell her?"

"The truth, as far as I know it. He was born in Maine, he was thirty when he died, and he had no people. At least, none that we've ever heard about."

I wasn't surprised that Bunny was pursuing her search. She had seen my reaction to finding the yellow shoebox. Living in Sugar Maple, the focus had always been on my mother Guinevere. My father had been an embarrassing addendum to Sugar Maple history, the human stain marring Aerynn's legacy and, as a result, mine as well.

For years I had thought little about the man my mother had loved enough to follow into eternity. I had willingly let him slip away into distant memory. But since Laria's birth, I had found myself longing to know more about the human who had been part of my life for such a short time. Watching Luke with our daughter awoke feelings I had long forgotten, feelings that escaped my control yesterday when I saw that battered yellow shoebox.

How was it possible to forget unconditional love?

No wonder Bunny's already formidable maternal instincts had gone into overdrive on my behalf.

"I doubt if she'll find anyone," I said, staring down at the glowing ring wedded to my index finger. "I'm thirty-two and nobody's ever come looking for me." At least, not so far.

"You never know who's out there," Lynette said. "I read a story the other day about two men who had been friends for over sixty years. One man never knew his father; the other had been adopted as an infant. So they were talking about that television show that traces a celebrity's family tree and they decided they would both take one of those DNA tests." She paused and took a sip of water. "Well, guess what? It turned out they were brothers!"

"Humans!" Midge Stallworth said with a surprising amount of disdain. "At least we never lose track of our bloodline."

"Of course you don't, dear," said Verna Griggs. "You just call it dinner."

Just another Knit Night at Sticks & Strings.

Chapter 7

GAVAN

Sugar Maple — one week before the wedding

HUMANS SMELLED like hot milk and spices. He hadn't expected that. He found himself inhaling their scent, alternately repelled and enchanted.

He moved quietly among them, invisible to their eyes, undetectable by their other senses. He felt their breath moving in and out of their fragile lungs, heard the rapid beating of more hearts than he could count. Their mortal force created eddies of heat around them, intersecting circles of life burning down like candles.

They were also loud, unpredictable, and everywhere. The only inviolate space was the waterfall portal where he had entered the dimension, and even then he could hear them moving swiftly along distant roads.

Even in Sugar Maple, the town created to give refuge to

magicks of all types, humans had left their mark. But it wasn't the mark of savagery and hate. They broke bread with the magicks and left their hard-earned money in their shops. The arrangement seemed to benefit both sides.

And nobody benefited more than Chloe of Guinevere. Her knit shop, situated in the center of town, was a thriving center of commerce and friendship. He watched through the front window of her store as she welcomed humans and magicks alike into her realm, treating each with warmth and humor as she plied her trade. He wasn't sure how many earth hours he spent that first day observing her at work but the sky went from light to nearly dark before she left.

Thanks to the new magick charm the Sugar Maples had settled over the town, the humans couldn't see him. Thanks to the old magick charm he had settled over himself, the Sugar Maples couldn't see him. He was free to observe without being detected.

He soon discovered there were limits to what he was comfortable observing.

The ring on his hand blinked each time he neared Chloe. Imbued with magick of its own, the ring seemed to know its destiny was on the horizon.

Standing outside the window of her cottage, he saw a family. He had communicated to Rohesia that his betrothed had created a child with the human, a beautiful baby girl who, despite being mostly human, exhibited a surprising degree of magick. A baby girl who would one day move Aerynn's legacy forward. Gavan needed no special powers to see that the three of them, magicks and human male, were bound together by love, the most powerful force in existence and maybe the most dangerous to his cause.

Rohesia remained unmoved. The plan would move forward and swiftly, per her original command.

The existence of one family for the survival of many.

There was no choice.

Chapter 8

WENDY AUBRY LATTIMER

Bailey's Harbor, Maine – three days before the wedding

IT WASN'T the craziest idea ever introduced in the Tip Top Coffee Shop but you wouldn't know it by the way my three best friends were looking at me.

"What?" I demanded as I dipped my fingers into the remains of my hot tea water and spit-spliced two strands of downy soft cashmere fingering weight together. "She asked. I said yes. What's the big deal?"

"It's a wedding invitation," Diandra said, her patience with me clearly strained. "Why would say yes to a wedding invitation? Haven't we all been to enough weddings by now?"

"Because the bride is my cousin," I said. "When a cousin asks, you say yes."

"Your cousin didn't ask you," Diandra reminded me.

"And she's a cousin you've never met," Kelly reminded me, "and never knew existed."

"A cousin who might not really be your cousin," Claire added. "All you have to go on is what this Bonny person has to say."

"Her name is Bunny and she's the bride's future mother-in-law."

"I can't believe we're even having this discussion," Diandra said as she slowly tinked her way back along a row of lace. "When I said you should get out there and meet someone, this isn't what I meant."

"I know exactly what you meant," I shot back, "and I'm still not ready."

"You've been divorced for almost a year. What are you waiting for?"

"Stop looking at me like I'm an exhibit in the Museum of Lost Women." I took another gulp of coffee. "When I'm ready to date, I'll let you know."

Diandra, Kelly, and Claire launched into their usual why-Wendy-should-put-down-her-knitting-and-pick-up-a-guy routine, most of which I knew by heart. They meant well, the three of them, but they all had great jobs, good husbands, and happy kids. We weren't all that lucky.

Don't get me wrong. I love those women. I mean, who else but your best girl friends would be there to pry the Ben & Jerry's from your cold, plump hands before you ate yourself into a post-divorce fat and sugar coma? But I'd be lying if I said I was anything like them. Sometimes I feel like their slacker mascot, a classic underachiever with only one husband, and one divorce and no children to my name.

I'm not a rocket scientist or an educator or a surgeon. I'm not even the "Do you want fries with that?" girl at

McDonald's. I clean other people's houses for a living and I knit for my sanity.

Some knitters knit for process. Some knit for product. I knit to keep from throwing myself under the vacuum cleaner.

I know how to keep a house looking great. It's one of the things I did well so when my life fell apart I figured why not make some money doing for others what I'd done for Gary for free. It's honest work. Maybe it's not what my parents had in mind when they shipped me off to college but neither was seeing me marry as soon as I was old enough to vote.

I suppose you want the juicy details. I can't really blame you for that. We all want to know how someone else's life fell apart, if only so we can hold on tighter to what's good about our own. What I thought would last forever lasted only until something better came along. He met someone younger, sexier, and richer and he divorced me and married her. I saw The New Wife once and I have to say if I weren't straight as a plumb line, I might have left me for her too.

And the sad truth is I never saw it coming.

One morning I was standing at the stove stirring the organic oatmeal and raisins concoction that had become our default breakfast when he sat down at the kitchen table, opened the paper to the classified section and said, "I'm moving out."

I thought he was kidding. I wish I could say I had one of those seen-it-coming moments but I didn't. I thought we were happy. I thought our family was like every other family out there in America: sometimes happy, sometimes not so much, but rock solid just the same.

Yeah.

I know.

You never think it can happen to you until it does and even then it took me a good six months to stop listening for the sound of his Miata in the driveway.

The thing is I liked being married. I liked the routine of it. The things that drove other women completely nuts were touchstones for me, reminders that I had a man who loved me and a place in the world where I belonged.

And then Hurricane Sophie blew into town and Barbie's Dream House came tumbling down before Barbie had a chance to figure out what came next.

Last week I learned that Gary and Sophie are expecting their first child and the pain cut through me like a machete. In some strange way I was happy for him. He had always wanted kids and that was the one thing I couldn't give him.

I guess sometimes dreams do come true.

Just not my dreams.

I'd been feeling restless lately, uneasy in my own skin. Dreams were wonderful but impossible dreams only weighed you down. Sooner or later I would have to step out of my comfort zone and jumpstart my life. This unexpected wedding invitation might be a great first step toward my second act. Whatever it might be.

"Are you finished?" I asked when my three BFFs stopped for breath. 'There's more to the story."

I handed Claire my iPad and leaned back.

"This better not be another picture of cute kittens and balls of yarn," she said, reluctantly turning the tablet toward her. "I swear I'll block you forever if you send me one more of those things."

"Just read the invitation."

I watched as her gaze traveled the screen.

"It's in Sugar Maple!" Claire all but shrieked. She passed the iPad to Kelly.

"Sticks-&-Strings Sugar Maple?" Kelly asked, wide-eyed.

She pushed it toward Diandra who remained unimpressed.

"Some chick sends you an email and you're racing over to Vermont to hold hands and sing Kumbaya with strangers. That doesn't sound like you, Wendy." She leaned across the table and fixed me with a look. "You know you don't need a wedding invitation to shop at Sticks & Strings. We've been talking about a road trip forever."

"I'm not a moron," I said, feeling slightly insulted. "I checked Bunny MacKenzie out."

She was a retired nurse from the Boston suburbs, married, with a boatload of kids and grandkids and a family that had more branches than the Rockefeller Center Christmas tree.

One of my half-sisters had asked me to compile information for a school project she was working on and, for a little while, I enjoyed filling in the names and watching as they linked up but that was as far as it went for me. I'm not a big family tree kind of girl. Maybe if I had children of my own, or even the possibility of children, I might find the search for family history more compelling, but that particular buck stopped with me. Janna had posted the results on-line at one of those ancestry websites, which was how Bunny MacKenzie had managed to track me down.

"Apparently Chloe Hobbs doesn't have any living relatives and Bunny was determined to find family to share her wedding day with her."

"Wait," Diandra said. "You're related to Chloe Hobbs? The owner of Sticks & Strings Chloe Hobbs?"

"That's what Bunny says." I probably sounded smug but who could blame me. According to Bunny, my father and Chloe's father had been second cousins which meant Chloe and I were cousins also, however many times removed.

Finding out that I was related to the owner of one of the most popular knit shops in the country was kind of cool. Okay, maybe not so much if you didn't have a serious jones for fiber, but I'll admit to a fangrrl flutter when I discovered I had a connection to the legendary shop where your yarn never tangles, your sleeves always turn out even, and you always get gauge.

"Family discount?" Claire asked, eyes twinkling with mischief.

"We can hope," I said.

I told them I planned to arrive the day before the wedding, so I would have time to meet Chloe and get in a little yarn shopping before the ceremony.

"Is the mother-in-law trying to screw with the bride?" Diandra asked. "I don't know about you, but I was barely sane the day before my wedding. A mystery cousin would've pushed me over the edge."

"Tell me about it." Kelly rolled her eyes. "If Dan's mother had pulled another relative out of her hat, I'd be serving time right now for manslaughter."

"Sorry, Wendy," Claire said, "but that is one terrible idea."

"Bunny says Chloe will be thrilled." I launched into the story I'd been told, how Chloe had grown up with no blood relatives and how much meeting me would mean to her.

Especially on the eve of her wedding day.

"'Especially on the eve of her wedding day'? Sounds like a load of crap to me," Diandra said, shaking her head.

It was starting to sound the same way to me. "I don't think Bunny's a liar," I said, wishing I felt more positive. "Misguided, maybe."

I'm not naïve. I know the world isn't filled with rainbows and unicorns. I was pretty certain the only thing Bunny was guilty of was bad judgment.

"It's only a three-hour drive," I said, as much for myself as for my friends. "I plan to arrive two days before the wedding. If we don't hit it off, I'll turn around and drive home and it will be like I was never there."

"Save yourself the gas money and we'll plan a weekend and go up there together," Claire said and the others nodded agreement.

"Great idea," I said, "but I'm still going to the wedding."

The groans were loud and long but I stood my ground. I needed to do this. I needed to get out of Bailey's Harbor and see who I was on my own, even if it was just for a handful of days.

"Just don't catch the bouquet and elope with a hot groomsman," Kelly said. "We intend to vet your next husband."

"I promise," I said, crossing my heart. "I'll be back before you even know I'm gone."

I was laughing as I drove out of the parking lot despite the odd feeling that instead of saying, "See you next week," I was really saying goodbye.

Chapter 9

CHLOE

Two days before the wedding

I HAD BEEN AT DAZZLE, the new dress shop owned by one of Lilith's sisters, since not long after daybreak, suffering through the final fitting of my wedding dress.

To be honest, I couldn't see why there was so much to fit. The dress was a simple sheath and I didn't exactly add a whole lot of curves to the underpinnings.

Well, at least not usually. Nursing had definitely made one area a whole lot more challenging.

"The dress looks fine," I said for probably the thousandth time. "The shoes are fine. Everything's fine. I need to go open up the shop."

Everyone ignored me.

"I'm not sure about the length," Bunny said, peering at

my reflection in the long mirror in front of me. "It needs to be a tad shorter."

"Shorter?" Lynette gave her a look. "It's too short by an inch. Her toes are peeking through."

"If it were up to me, I'd say tea length." Luke's Aunt Peggy wasn't shy about sharing her opinions even though she had the fashion sense of a cloistered nun.

His sister Meghan rolled her eyes. "If I had Chloe's legs, I'd go for a micro mini."

Janice wasn't about to be left out. "I'd ditch the white and go for some color."

"Any more unsolicited advice and I'll show up in jeans and a t-shirt," I warned them. "I'm going to send Luke a selfie and see what he thinks."

The word "NO!" exploded in the room like cannon fire. This was clearly a subject both magicks and mortals could agree on.

"Are you nuts?" Lynette shrieked. "That's begging for trouble!"

"You never *ever* let the groom see the dress before the wedding day." Bunny made it sound like it was the eleventh commandment.

"I guess I don't have the bride gene," I said with a shrug.

"You'd better find it and fast," Isolda, Lilith's sister, said as she fussed with the hem of the dress. "In forty-eight hours you're going to be the main attraction."

The mystery ring on my index finger began to glow more brightly and I thrust my hand behind my back. It had been glowing warm and bright at sporadic intervals that had me both puzzled and uneasy. The charms we had wrapped around it no longer shielded its glimmer from curious human eyes.

"You really need to do something about that ring." Of course Bunny had noticed. "It's too distracting."

"Bunny's right," Lilith, who should have known better, said. "It will detract from your wedding ring after you and Luke exchange vows."

"I know, I know." I was unable to hide my exasperation. "Soap, butter, axle grease--we've tried everything short of an acetylene torch. It won't budge."

Bunny shook her head. "I still don't understand how such a huge ring ended up such a tight fit. When you first took it out of the box, I would have sworn it would be too big on Gronk."

I had grown accustomed to Bunny's occasional football references by now and just nodded in agreement.

"Did you try icing your hand?"

"Bunny, I've tried everything. I'll probably make an appointment with an orthopedist after the wedding and have it sawed off." Preferably by someone who knew how to do it without causing bodily harm.

"Well, it just doesn't go with your dress."

"Duly noted," I said.

Was it too late to elope?

The chatter went on around me non-stop. I disappeared into the changing room to slip back into my jeans and a summery knit tee I'd whipped up last week when a remark caught my attention.

"...peeping tom!"

I poked my head out through the curtains. "Did someone say peeping tom?" Up until that moment, I'd only heard that phrase in the old movies I loved.

A burst of laughter greeted my question.

"Don't call the cop," Meghan said, referencing her brother who was the sum total of our police force.

More laughter.

I fastened the waistband of my jeans and joined them again.

"Are you saying Sugar Maple has a peeping tom?"

"I'm not saying we do or we don't," Isolda replied as she carefully laid my beautiful dress on her spacious worktable. She shrugged her elegant shoulders and glanced toward her sister Lilith. "Right now, it's nothing more than a feeling."

I frowned. "What kind of feeling?"

"What else?" Janice said, feigning an offhanded manner. "Like we're being watched."

I glanced around the room filled with dear friends and almost-family. I had almost asked, "By mortal or magick?" but caught myself just in time. "You've all felt it?" I asked instead.

Meghan shook her head no. Lynette said, "Me neither."

But everyone else had something to add.

"I was closing the curtains last night at the Inn," Bunny said, "and I'd almost swear I heard someone breathing outside the window."

"Did you actually see anything?" I asked. "Deer? Bear? Maybe a giant squirrel?"

She gave me the kind of look that had probably stopped her kids in their tracks back in the day. "I grew up in a small farming town, Chloe. I know all about wildlife."

I mumbled an apology and she gave me a hug.

Janice had sensed a presence outside the window of the hair salon. Lilith had the feeling someone had been lurking at her bedroom window. Luke's Aunt Peggy had taken her bath in the dark after the bushes underneath her window at the Inn rustled.

Either they were all hallucinating or something was going on and as *de facto* mayor, I needed to find out more. I know this sounds terrible, but maybe I could postpone dealing with the peeping tom until after the wedding. Seventy-two hours from now, the MacKenzie clan would be back home and I could poke around without worrying that I'd expose any of our secrets.

Besides, I had a pretty good idea who was doing the peeping. The Souderbushes, a Sugar Maple family of ghosts, spent much of their time traveling the Spirit Trail. With the wedding embargo in place, their three eternally-teenage boys had a lot of time on their hands.

You do the math.

I would, however, run it by Luke. (If I remembered. I definitely had a bad case of bride brain by now.)

We finally broke up a little before noon and went off to our various jobs and responsibilities. I felt like I'd run a marathon and lost. A group of MacKenzies headed out in search of a mall but Bunny stuck close as glue, tapping away on her smartphone. I opened the door to Sticks & Strings just in time to greet the UPS driver.

"Big day coming up, Chloe," he said, depositing two huge boxes of Noro's latest fiber masterpiece. "You gettin' nervous?"

"A little bit, Tony. I'll save you some cake."

"Everyone is so nice up here," Bunny said, pocketing her smartphone as the front door chimed behind him. "Even your UPS drivers. Not the way we are in Boston."

"We have our share of cranks," I said with a little more snark than I'd intended.

Bunny laughed. "Like that Verna woman?"

"Excellent example," I said, laughing for the first time all morning. "And Midge Stallworth is right there with her."

Bunny feigned a shudder. "I don't know what it is with that little woman, but she gives me the creeps. Every time I see her, I feel like she's measuring me for a casket."

"Join the club," I said. "She gives us all the creeps."

I opened blinds, checked the thermostat on the central air, started the coffee, and generally got the shop ready for business.

Penelope, store cat and beloved companion, was exactly where I knew she'd be: nestled deep into the basket of self-replenishing roving that rested by the side of the fireplace. Both Penny and the roving had a centuries-long history with Hobbs women. Legend had it Penny had belonged to my ancestor Aerynn and had followed her when Aerynn led the other magicks from Salem in search of safety from persecution. Down through the years, Penny had remained a loyal companion to a succession of Hobbs women.

Sometimes she'd even been known to pull a certain Hobbs out of a very sticky situation.

Not that I'd know anything about that, you understand.

"What can I do to help?" Bunny asked, glancing around the shop. "Do you want me to unload the boxes?"

"Absolutely not! I'm just going to slide them into the storeroom and worry about them after the wedding."

"There must be something I can do for you."

"You don't have to hang out with me, Bunny," I said. "I love the company but I know you have a spa appointment with Janice."

"That's not until two o'clock. I have plenty of time."

I was starting to get suspicious.

"I'm surprised you didn't go to the mall with the others," I remarked casually.

"I'd rather spend time with you."

My suspicions went up a notch. Nobody loved malls more than Bunny MacKenzie.

"You do know the baby is at home with Elspeth today, right?"

"I'm here to spend time with you, Chloe, not the baby."

"Okay," I said, hands planted on hips. "What's going on?"

"Nothing." The twinkle in her eyes belied her innocent demeanor. "I don't know what you're talking about."

"Bunny, we both know you're up to something. Tell me what's going on."

She polished off the last of her coffee.

"Remember when I told you that I'd added you and Laria to the MacKenzie family tree?"

"Yes," I said, very carefully. "Lilith said you texted her with a few questions about my father's background."

"You make it sound so nefarious," she said with a slightly nervous laugh. "Just name, birth date, that sort of thing."

"Where is this going, Bunny? You're making me nervous."

"I found a birth certificate for your dad, but nothing anywhere for your mom. Are you sure she was born here in Sugar Maple?"

"Positive." I hated this more with every second. "We were supposed to digitize our records for the state. Lilith must have sent all of the raw data away to be processed."

"Anyway, that's neither here nor there right now." She

was beaming with pleasure as she met my eyes. "I found your cousin Wendy and invited her to the wedding."

I stared at her blankly. "I don't have a cousin Wendy." Or a cousin Joe, Mary, or John. I had no brothers, no sisters, no cousins, no uncles, no aunts, no nieces, no nephews. Except for Laria and Luke, my family tree was nothing but a stump.

Bunny gave me one of those funny little MacKenzie smiles I still hadn't quite managed to translate. "Actually you do," Bunny said. "Her name is Wendy Aubry Lattimer and she's from Maine, same as your dad."

It turned out your blood really can run cold inside your veins. I had never believed it could happen until now. The sound of my father's surname sent an icy shockwave through my body that almost dropped me to my knees.

I struggled to keep it together.

"I can't believe you invited a total stranger to the wedding."

"She's not a stranger, honey, she's your cousin."

"A cousin I've never met." And didn't know existed until thirty seconds ago.

Bunny's smile grew even wider. "She's probably at the Inn right now, checking in."

My mind exploded with the eight thousand things that could go wrong, all of which had to do with exposing Sugar Maple's secret to the rest of the world.

Words failed me. At least, the kind of words that wouldn't get me arrested.

"She's a knitter," Bunny offered with a cheerful if slightly forced smile. I think I was making her nervous, even though that wasn't my intention. "You should have heard her when I said that yes, you were the Chloe from Sticks & Strings."

I tried to be happy about this new relative, but big black clouds of doom were rolling toward me from every direction. "I really wish you hadn't done this, Bunny. This was supposed to be for immediate family and close friends."

"And she's your family, honey." She gave me one of her wonderful, warm hugs. "I wanted you and Laria to connect with your own blood relatives. I prayed that I'd find one of your kin to join us for the celebration. I've been hunting for awhile and I'd all but given up hope."

"It's not that I don't appreciate all you did to find this Wendy person--"

"Wendy Lattimer."

I nodded "Wendy Lattimer. But does it have to be right now? The wedding is the day after tomorrow!"

"That's exactly why I did it. Weddings are about joining families together."

I might have spent the first thirty years of my life as a mortal but that didn't mean I understood them.

A normal bride-to-be would be happy. A normal bride-to-be would hug her future mother-in-law and cry with joy. This bride-to-be wanted to pull a Superman and turn back time to before said mother-in-law knew how to use the internet.

"I'm so excited," Bunny said as she poured us each a giant mug of freshly-brewed coffee. "I feel like I've really gotten to know Wendy over the last ten days. You two are going to love each other."

Bunny was a people person in the truest sense of the phrase. She thrived on interaction with relatives, friends, strangers and all of her on-line friends. The thought of meeting my distant cousin had her buzzing with the kind of excitement a kid feels at Christmas.

I couldn't afford to love cousin Wendy. I couldn't afford to even get to know her. I'd spent most of my life wishing I had a blood relative to call my own and now here I was wishing said relative would stay far away from Sugar Maple.

My life was different now. My primary concern was the safety of Luke and Laria and my Sugar Maple family. Nothing else mattered. It was, after all, why I existed. Why I had been born. My purpose was to continue what my ancestor Aerynn had started here in Sugar Maple: maintaining a place where the different, the Other, could live in peace and harmony with the mortal world. Even if it took a fair bit of magick and camouflage to achieve, it was a worthwhile goal and one that was my destiny.

The world was growing smaller and more connected with each day that passed. Hiding in plain sight had never been easy, but now, when drones and satellites recorded your every move, it was almost impossible. We had fought hard to keep Sugar Maple on this side of the mist not too long ago, and I was afraid the day was coming when we would lose that battle.

I inhaled deeply and plunged ahead. "So what do you know about her?"

Bunny visibly relaxed. "As I said, her name is Wendy Aubry Lattimer. Her husband left her for a younger woman about two years ago. She's just shy of thirty. Divorced. No kids."

"What does she do for a living?"

"She cleans houses."

"She owns a company?"

"She owns a mop and a vacuum cleaner. No other employees."

"You said she's a knitter."

"Obsessive. She intends to buy out the shop."

I rolled my eyes "I've heard that before. Everyone says they're going to swoop up all the yarn they can carry, but one look at the price tag on a merino-silk hand-painted sock-weight and suddenly they go running back to Red Heart."

"You sound cynical, Chloe. That's not like you."

"I'm not cynical," I said. "Just realistic."

She patted my hand. "I'm thinking that maybe you're a little bit scared to open yourself up."

Damn it. My eyes filled with tears. That part of my life, the part where I'd had two parents who loved me, had been closed for almost as along as I could remember. I wasn't sure how I felt about opening the door and letting in both the light and the shadows.

"My father has been on my mind a lot since Laria was born. Watching Luke with her brings back some memories I thought were long gone." Sometimes they hurt like hell.

"Good memories?"

"The best." Six years with him weren't a lot to go on but it was all I had.

Maybe I wasn't just worried about magick, after all. Apparently the human part of my heart had a few concerns of its own.

Chapter 10

WENDY

Sugar Maple Inn

"SORRY, but we don't have any rooms available." The clerk behind the desk at the Sugar Maple Inn flashed me a movie-star smile. "We're hosting a private event this weekend and we're full up."

"Chloe Hobbs's wedding on Saturday," I said, flashing my own less-impressive smile back at her. "That's why I'm here."

"You're with the MacKenzie party?" The woman's extraordinary purple-blue eyes narrowed slightly. "I thought I had all the names."

"Bunny MacKenzie invited me, but I'm actually on the bride's side."

"The bride's side?" The woman's tone grew a tad less friendly. "I know everyone on the bride's side."

"Well, now you do," I said, a tad less friendly myself. "So do you have an available room or not?"

She excused herself and disappeared into the room adjacent to the check-in desk. I heard a volley of words, none of which I could make out, then the clerk reappeared with an older version of herself by her side.

"I'm Renate Weaver, one of the owners of the Inn," the older woman said pleasantly, extending a perfectly-manicured hand toward me. "My daughter says you're looking for a room."

It was like shaking cotton candy. I quickly pulled my hand away. (I have a thing about fluffy handshakes.) "I know it's short notice, but Bunny only invited me a few days ago." I made one of those what-can-you-do gestures and forced a smile.

The two women exchanged glances.

"So you're a MacKenzie."

"No. I'm a Lattimer by marriage, an Aubry by birth." I was starting to get a little annoyed. "Do you have a room for me or not?"

"You're an Aubry?" Renate asked, looking a shade paler than she had moments ago.

"Was an Aubry," I said, "but I don't see why that's so—"

"You're one of Chloe's people!" She said it like I'd announced I was the living embodiment of Bigfoot.

"Second cousin, twice removed." Or something like that. The degrees between relatives always turned my brain to mush.

"Are you sure?"

"I'm asking for a room, not government clearance." I adjusted my crossbody bag. "Thanks for the help. I'll stay somewhere else."

I turned to leave but a feather-soft touch on the arm stopped me.

"I'm so sorry," Renate said. "It's just that we're a very small inn and there are a lot of MacKenzies coming to town for the event. We promised we could accommodate them and it's been quite the task. I never expected anyone from Chloe's side to show up."

The younger woman, Renate's clone, nodded vigorously. "I mean, we all know she has no family of her own."

Bunny had mentioned that in passing but it hadn't registered until now.

"I understand," I said, "but I think I'll stay elsewhere just the same." Motel 6 was starting to sound like the Four Seasons to me.

"No!" Renate sounded downright insulted. "If we can find room for Luke's people, we can definitely find room for Chloe's."

"I'm not Chloe's people," I corrected her, feeling increasingly uncomfortable. Just a very distant relative who should have known better than to show up at the wedding of a cousin she'd never met.

The younger woman came around the front desk and I tried hard not to stare. She looked like a very short supermodel in skinny jeans and a tank top. What was in Sugar Maple's water anyway? These people were freaking gorgeous.

"Are these your bags?" She pointed toward the two small soft-sided pieces at my feet.

The question seemed rhetorical given the fact I was the only customer in the room, but I nodded anyway. There were times when a girl has to suppress her inner wiseass.

She picked them up like they weighed nothing which, to

be honest, they did. One was empty, the other almost empty. More room for all the yarn I hoped to buy.

"Why don't you take a walk around town?" Renate suggested, a bright smile on her movie-star gorgeous face. "If you're hungry, I can recommend Fully Caffeinated."

"The paninis are to die for," said the younger woman.

"You promise you'll find me a room? I don't want to hang around for no reason."

Renate beamed a high wattage smile. "Guaranteed."

GAVAN

THE DRESS SHOP where he had observed Chloe and her companions was diagonally across from the Inn. A small metal box with wheels (they called it a car) rumbled up to the front door of the Inn and a tall dark-haired woman got out. Her resemblance to Chloe caught his attention immediately. Although her hair was darker, she carried herself with the same disarming blend of confidence and human insecurity that he had observed in the female to whom he was betrothed.

The gathering at the dress shop ended with the women, mortal and magick, waving goodbye as they headed off in different directions. He had intended to continue shadowing Chloe as she moved through her day, but this new human intrigued him. She was an unexpected complication who deserved close observation.

The woman entered the Inn and he followed behind her,

trusting that his magick, unfamiliar to the inhabitants of Sugar Maple, would continue to conceal his presence.

This female was clearly mortal. The Fae owners of the Inn seemed reluctant to give her shelter, which confirmed that fact. While they maintained a pleasant and hospitable demeanor, it was clear they wanted no part of her or of her business. Even when she revealed herself to be part of Chloe's blood kin, they were slow to relent.

Did they sense danger in her presence? He was new to this dimension. He was not yet able to understand the signifiers that seemed obvious to the inhabitants. He had not bargained on a human blood link to his betrothed and he determined to make sure she would not get in his way.

She exhibited anger when she left the Inn. It showed in the tight lines of her face and the way she seemed to attack the sidewalk with each step. So he had not imagined the hostility. Her reaction confirmed it for him.

He shadowed her as she made her way up the street. He hoped she would climb back into that little metal machine in which she had arrived and roll away from Sugar Maple. Unfortunately, his hopes were dashed when she opened the door to a place called Fully Caffeinated and stepped inside.

Instantly he knew that mortals were in the minority. As far as he could tell, she might be the only one present. The high magick energies circulating around the large room worried him. He was not ready for his presence to be recognized. Not until he had gathered the facts he needed.

This time he would watch from the other side of the big wall of glass.

WENDY

FULLY CAFFEINATED WAS on the corner of Osborne and Bishop, a short walk from the Inn. It was one of those perfect late August days that come around maybe once every ten years: sunny, warm but not hot, a gentle breeze rustling through the trees. It was the kind of day that brings people out of their houses to enjoy the weather, but the only sign of life in Sugar Maple was the occasional car rolling by.

No young mothers chatting while they pushed double strollers. No kids tearing down the sidewalk on their way to the park. No old people perched on a park bench watching the world go by.

Just me.

Weird.

Did you ever go on one of those Hollywood studio tours where they take you onto the back lots? A road in ancient Rome presses up against a High Street in Dickensian London, which fights a row of Manhattan brownstones for room. The sets are perfectly rendered, right down to cigarette butts on the sidewalk but that was where it ended. Peek around the corner and you'd find nothing but scaffolding and dreams.

That was how Sugar Maple made me feel.

I like neat and orderly as well as the next person. (Maybe more, considering the fact that I clean houses for a living.) But there was a real Stepford feeling to the place that unnerved me.

One night here would be more than enough.

I pushed open the door to Fully Caffeinated and stopped in my tracks. The noise was deafening. Maybe this was why the streets were so empty. Everyone in town was in the coffee shop, talking at the tops of their lungs.

I placed my order up front then claimed a lone seat near the back door and pulled my phone from my crossbody bag.

"Where are you?" Diandra didn't bother with hello. "It sounds like you're in the middle of a bee hive."

"A coffee shop in Sugar Maple. It does better business than the Tip Top."

"So how do you like the town? Is it as great as they say on Yelp?"

"Jury's out. So far I'm not impressed."

A woman two seats over shot me a look that brought me up short. I didn't think I'd been speaking that loud but maybe I had.

"I need details," Diandra said.

"Later," I said as a server deposited my turkey club in front of me. "I just wanted you to know I made it in one piece. I'll text you after I meet the cousin."

The turkey club was great. They served it with a bottomless basket of homemade potato chips that were sinfully delicious. Funny how judicious applications of fat and salt can soothe a woman's jangled nerves.

A very round woman with a mop of curls sat down next to me. I couldn't help noticing that her feet didn't touch the ground.

"You should have ordered the panini," she said without preamble. "Henry is known for his paninis."

Good for Henry. "The turkey club is excellent."

She made a dismissive gesture. "If you like club sandwiches."

"Actually I do," I said. "That's why I ordered it."

"To each her own," the woman said. "But next time try a panini."

I gave her my best noncommittal smile then took another bite of my turkey club and looked down at my phone.

She didn't take the hint.

"Are you here for the wedding?"

I nodded, grateful that my mouth was full.

She scanned my face like she was the head of airport security. "You don't look like a MacKenzie."

I swallowed then took a sip of iced tea. "I'm not."

"A friend of theirs?"

I shook my head. "Not really." Clearly she would keep on asking so I might as well tell her. "I'm related to Chloe."

"No, you're not."

"Actually I am."

"Chloe doesn't have any – you should excuse the expression – blood relations."

"She has me."

"No offense, but I don't believe you."

"None taken, but it's true." I took another huge bite of turkey club. "Ask Bunny MacKenzie. She's the one who is bringing Chloe and me together."

A lean woman with a stern face joined Squeaky at the tiny round table.

"Verna Griggs," she said with a terse nod in my direction. "Who are you?"

Good thing I was a New Englander, born and bred. Somebody else might have been offended.

"Wendy Lattimer," I said.

"Coast of Maine," she said.

"Good call. Most people think Boston."

"Most people don't have my ear for accents."

"Do you live here?" I asked.

"Ten generations," she said, "and more coming up behind me."

"Twelve generations," Squeaky chimed in, not to be outdone. "Did I mention I'm Midge Stallworth. My husband and I own the funeral parlor up the street."

I must have involuntarily recoiled because she laughed out loud.

"Don't worry," she said with another one of those squeaky laughs. "I'm not looking to drum up more business."

Verna shot her a look that would have made me run for the hills. I wondered what that was about. It sounded like pretty standard funeral home humor to me.

"What brings you to Sugar Maple?" Verna asked. No offense, but the woman must have missed a few waxing sessions lately. Her brows not only met over the bridge of her nose, they married.

"She's here for Chloe's wedding," Midge said with an arch of her left brow. "Isn't that wonderful?"

"Another MacKenzie," Verna said, shaking her head. "I should have known."

"Wrong!" Midge crowed with obvious delight before I could say a word. "She's not a MacKenzie." She paused for what seemed to me unnecessary dramatic effect. "She's related to Chloe."

The room fell silent.

I'm not exaggerating when I say you could have heard a pin drop three towns away. Every eye in the place turned toward me. Every ear wagged in my direction.

I started babbling something about DNA tests and my

half-sister Janna and how it somehow connected with Bunny's family tree project but I had the distinct feeling no one was listening.

Let me clarify that: they weren't listening to me, but I was pretty sure they were talking about me. Not that I could hear them, but it felt like at least a dozen silent conversations were going on all around me. I know that sounds crazy. I mean the coffee shop was dead quiet but I would have bet my Toyota that messages were being sent and received. You could almost see words ricocheting off each other as they flew around the room like a mob of startled crows.

My turkey club had lost its appeal. I reached into my wallet and pulled out a few bills and laid the tip by my plate.

"It's been nice, ladies," I said, pushing back my chair and standing up. "I'll see you tomorrow at the wedding."

"Sticks & Strings is around the corner," Midge Stallworth squeaked as I strode across the coffee shop. "But I'll bet you already knew that."

I thanked her for the information but I was pretty sure I would have found it anyway. I can smell yarn from a hundred yards away and the unmistakable scents of Bluefaced Leicester, angora, merino, Lopi, and every other glorious combination of fibers were already filling my head.

Okay, so maybe I have a good imagination but it wasn't every day I got to visit a world-class shop that happened to be owned by a distant relative.

And yes, the thought of a fifty-percent-off family discount had occurred to me, even if it was beginning to lose its appeal.

Once outside I took a moment to orient myself. The grid was pretty simple with the tourist area all within a two-block rectangle. I struck out for Sticks & Strings at a brisk gait.

GAVAN

CURRENTS OF ENERGY followed her out the door and down the street. Once again she had not been welcomed by the magicks, not even when they learned she shared a bloodline with Chloe. Behind their smiles and laughter, they sensed danger and he would heed their warning.

The world had evolved since his clan had lived among them but the distrust between mortals and magicks still burned like a fire that could not be extinguished.

He understood the fears that beat inside the magicks' hearts at the thought of yet another human living among them. Beneath the surface, fear of humans lived and breathed, same as it had when his clan went beyond the mist.

He would not hurt the human called Wendy, but he would send a signal that she would be unwise to ignore.

WENDY

ACCORDING TO MY GUIDEBOOK, most of the families in Sugar Maple could trace their roots back to the late seventeenth century when Sugar Maple was still known by an impossible-to-pronounce Native American name. That could explain the clannish feeling I'd sensed at Fully Caffeinated but I felt it went deeper than that.

There was something weird about the town, apart from the number of beautiful people, but I couldn't quite put my figure on exactly what.

Once again the streets were pedestrian-free. A UPS truck rolled slowly by, stopping at the corner sign, then continuing on its way. There was no movement except for a light breeze rustling the leaves and lifting my bangs from my forehead.

I was alone.

Except that I wasn't. I could feel eyes on me, probably peering from behind the curtained windows that lined the street. For a town that was supported by tourism, they seemed uncomfortable having a stranger in their midst.

Which made zero sense no matter how you parsed it. The town was supported one hundred percent by tourists hungry for a taste of Norman Rockwell's New England and maybe a few skeins of kettle-dyed yarn. There were no manufacturing plants in Sugar Maple. No high tech companies to drive their economy. They should be welcoming tourists with open arms, not nosy questions.

Then again, maybe I was the only one they were having trouble with.

They had all been adamant in their belief that Chloe had no blood relatives, almost aggressively so, as if the idea threatened them in some way. Ridiculous? Maybe it was. But so was deciding to show up at a stranger's wedding at the request of another stranger.

What in hell had I been thinking?

What if my friends were right and Bunny MacKenzie was wrong and there was no blood link between Chloe and me? What if she'd gotten her facts wrong and Chloe and I were part of totally different Aubry families? As far as I knew, Chloe hadn't had her DNA tested so there was no scientific basis for claiming a family relationship.

No wonder Claire and Diandra and Kelly had looked at me like I'd suddenly gone crazy. I had no proof at all of actual kinship (however distant) beyond the snooping abilities of a retired nurse from Boston.

Go home.

I stopped in my tracks. We all have that little voice in our heads, the one that pops up when you least expect it, and tells you what to do. Like most people, I usually ignore it but this time was different.

It wasn't my voice I was hearing. It was a man's voice.

And yet there was no one there.

Go home.

I spun around again.

Still nothing.

Talk about a welcoming committee.

The jury was no longer out.

I didn't like Sugar Maple and it was beginning to look like Sugar Maple didn't like me. Call me crazy, but something weird was going on and I didn't want to be part of it.

Not even for yarn at a family discount.

If I left now, I could be home before dark. All I had to do was go back to the Inn, grab my bags, and point my car toward Maine.

Which turned out to be easier said than done.

Maybe I would just take a look at the front window of Sticks & Strings before I left. I mean, what knitter worth her stash could get this close to fiber nirvana without at least a peek at paradise.

Besides, nobody knew what I looked like. Even if Bunny MacKenzie was standing there looking back at me, she'd think I was just your average window shopper.

The window display was quirky and compelling. Lots of funky fleeces, baskets of roving, and swoony, summery shawls interspersed with serious hand-painted yarnage with antique spinning wheels suspended from the ceiling. I could feel my hard-earned money trying to escape from my wallet.

I leaned a little closer to see if I could spot any life beyond the window display, but the sun's reflection off the glass made it hard to see beyond the glare. I felt a rush of air near my left ear and I turned quickly but there was no one there. I chalked it up to the Sugar-Maple-is-weird factor.

Still I had the strongest feeling that I wasn't alone even though I was the only one on the street. You know how it feels when someone invades your personal space? How even the tiny hairs on your arms register another presence? That was how I felt as I surveyed the display at Sticks & Strings.

And then I saw him.

He was standing just behind my left shoulder. The glare from the sun reflecting off the window made it impossible to see his face in the reflection. He was tall, broad shouldered, clad in (of all things) a dark cape with some kind of red and orange embroidery across the front. He seemed to be shadowing me, blocking my view of – well, of everything but him.

"Hey!" I said. "Give a girl some space."

I spun around to get a better look at the pushy stranger but there was nothing but empty space where he had been.

I turned back to the window display and there he was again, reflected over my right shoulder this time, his face still in shadow. This time his arms were outstretched, like a giant bird shielding me with the wings of his cloak.

Or maybe trying to kill me.

I had taken a few self-defense courses. I knew what to do. I spun around, ready to deliver a well-placed knee to an unprotected groin and kept right on spinning.

Chapter 11

CHLOE

THROWING your future mother-in-law out of your yarn shop probably wasn't the wisest thing to do on the day before your wedding, but Bunny seemed to understand it wasn't anything personal.

I needed space. I'm not sure Wyoming would have been enough space for me, but I'd take what I could get at this point, but the last twenty minutes of alone time was a start.

I was still reeling from my experience with the Book of Spells at the library. The hideous images I'd seen still lingered, ferocious and terrifying, at the edges of my consciousness, waiting to grab me. How any of that figured in with the glowing ring that seemed permanently attached to my finger was anyone's guess. And I mean anyone's, because so far nobody in Sugar Maple had a clue.

Luke was off having lunch with his father, brothers, and

brothers-in-law. Some kind of ersatz bachelor party, I assumed. I texted him an update on Bunny's latest left-field surprise and his response was short and right on the mark.

WTH?

AS FAR AS I was concerned, that pretty much summed up the last few weeks.

I paced the shop, unable to settle down. I didn't want to knit or spin or check stock. Social media held little appeal. All I could think about was this mystery cousin Bunny had found on-line. What would she be like? Would she like me? Would I like her? Had she known my father?

Was she at Fully Caffeinated, chowing down on a panini or (I admit I was pulling hard for this one) had she decided to jump back in her car and head for home?

Maybe heading home was what I should do. The experience with the Book of Spells yesterday had exhausted me. I had laid awake most of the night trying to make sense of the horrors I'd seen, to figure out how they tied in with the mini earthquake, the ring, the general sense that something bad was coming. And let's not even start on the figure in the cape with the gorgeous Welsh embroidery on it and the pull I felt toward him.

I checked on Penny the cat, made sure she had food and water and that the a/c was working the way it should. The stupid ring was suddenly blinking for reasons unknown but I didn't have the time or inclination to worry about it now. I was about to gather up my things and head out when I heard a loud thump near the front door to the shop. Birds sometimes hit the plate glass window, stunning themselves into immobility, but this sounded more substantial.

Moving swiftly, I crossed the room then flung open the door, yelping in surprise when a woman tumbled into the shop.

"I've always had a knack for the grand entrance," she said, looking up at me with huge brown eyes that seemed vaguely familiar. "Falling over my own feet is my specialty."

Whoever she was, I liked her immediately. "I thought I had that specialty all wrapped up." I was known in Sugar Maple as a major klutz.

"You've met your match." She rolled those big brown eyes and made a face. "Good thing I have strong bones."

"Are you hurt?"

"Just my pride," she said. "I was aiming for a clean getaway."

Just like that I knew who she was. "You're Wendy, aren't you?"

"Guilty." She flashed a quick smile. "And you're Chloe."

I nodded. "So why were you looking to get away?"

"Let's just say your future mother-in-law is way too persuasive. This was a stupid idea and I should have known better. I figured I'd come back some other time." Her smile widened. "Like maybe when you're not getting married."

I didn't argue the point. "Let me help you up."

I held out my hand and she took it. Her fingers were long and bony like mine. I noticed she didn't wear a wedding ring and I tried to remember what Bunny had said about her marital status.

"Count of three," I said. "One, two—"

"Ow!" She fell back down on her butt. "I think I might have sprained my ankle."

"Okay," I said. "No problem. We'll get you into the shop so we can have a look."

She winced as we made another attempt. "Just don't let me buy anything."

"No promises," I said, as she leaned her weight against me and hobbled inside. "I am, after all, a professional fiber enabler."

She laughed but I could see she was hurting. Any attempt to put weight on her right foot caused her to emit a small groan.

I helped her to the maple rocking chair near my favorite antique wheel and she sank onto it with a grateful sigh. I knelt in front of her and looked at her right ankle. It was already starting to swell.

"On a scale of one to ten, how bad is it?" I asked.

She thought for a second. "Low seven."

I whistled. "Low sevens for me mean full body anesthesia. I'll get some ice."

Penny roused herself from her basket of roving and wandered over to check out the newcomer. By the time I returned with towels and a bucket of ice, Penny was ensconced on Wendy's lap.

"I hope you're a cat person," I said, resuming my position on the floor in front of her. "As you can see, Penny doesn't wait to be asked."

"Cats, dogs, birds, ferrets, hamsters, I love them all."

"Good to know." I reached for her ankle. "This might hurt. Tell me if you want me to stop."

She nodded. I saw her lips thin the slightest bit as I rested her right foot on a pillow.

"Sorry," I said. "I promise the ice will help." I wrapped the makeshift ice pack around her ankle.

"You're good at this," she said. "Do you have nursing training like Bunny?"

"Experience," I said. "I'm no stranger to tripping over my own feet."

A funny look passed across her even features. "About that fall," she began. "There was this guy—"

I rocked back on my heels and looked up at her. "I didn't see anybody."

"It was weird," she said, stretching out her leg and looking down at her swollen ankle. "I was on my way here when I suddenly decided that maybe this wasn't the greatest time to pop up for a visit. But I couldn't be this close to Sticks & Strings and not at least peek in the window." She stopped. "It sounds ridiculous, I know it does, but there was a . . . figure lurking behind me."

"Lurking?"

"Okay, here is where it gets weird," she said. "I saw his reflection in the store window but when I turned around, there was nobody there."

I didn't like this at all. Either she was certifiable or the charm I'd settled on Sugar Maple for the wedding was fading fast. Frankly, I was hoping for crazy. "Then what happened?"

"I turned back to the window and there he was again, but on my other side. I still couldn't see his face, but this time his arms were raised and with that crazy embroidered cloak and everything—"

"A cloak?" I couldn't keep the shock from my voice. "A cloak in August?" The significance was just out of reach.

"I know, right? I guess I freaked out and spun around to knee him in the groin and—" She made a helpless gesture with her hands. "I kept right on spinning."

This was getting worse by the second. "And what did this mystery man do while you were spinning like a top?"

"Nothing. Like I said, I never really saw him, except for the reflection in the window."

"Did he say anything to you?"

She hesitated. "No, but when I first rounded the corner on my way here, I thought I heard a voice tell me to go home."

"Male or female?"

She looked so embarrassed that I hated myself for asking.

"It was just one of those little voices in your head," she said. "I know I must sound crazy."

"Male or female?" I asked again.

"Male," she said. "Definitely male."

"Tell me more about the mystery man," I said. "Are you sure you didn't see his face?"

"Positive."

"What was so compelling about him? Describe what happened the best you can."

Wendy's expression grew wary. "I thought your future husband was the detective. I'm starting to feel like I need a lawyer."

"Sorry," I said with an embarrassed laugh. "I'm not a detective, but I am the mayor of Sugar Maple and you were hurt within our town limits. I want to make sure we don't have a problem." The poor woman looked like I was about to Mirandize her.

Her expression softened but I sensed she was more on guard than she had been earlier which made me feel terrible. "There's not much to describe. I probably took too many self-defense courses. Like I said before, I spun around and I must have hit something, because I lost my balance and spun myself right onto my butt."

"And he didn't try to help you?"

"He was gone." She hesitated for a moment. "At least his reflection was gone. I'm starting to think I imagined the whole thing."

We agreed that bright sunlight and reflective glass were an interesting combination. I'm not sure either one of us believed a word we were saying but at least we were trying.

A rush of memory knocked the breath out of me. "Tell me more about that cloak. I'm a needlework junkie. I need to know these things."

"A dragon," she said. "Very upscale Comic Con with lots of fiery reds and oranges. I wish I could've gotten a better look at it. Actually the whole image was pretty compelling even without seeing his face. We don't have anyone like that in Bailey's Harbor."

I had felt the same pull when the man from the Book of Spells walked through the fire.

"I sound like a real loony, don't I?" she asked.

"I once sold angora to a woman who claimed she liked to eat it on toast with marmalade. We set a pretty high bar for loony around here."

She nodded. "I noticed. The women at the café weren't exactly the friendliest group. I half expected a drone to do some fly-by surveillance."

I readjusted the ice wrap around her ankle. "Was a short, round little woman named Midge at Fully Caffeinated?"

"Yes!" Wendy's face lit up. "And a stern, schoolmarm type—darn! I can't remember her name."

"Verna Griggs," I said. "I'd bet the yarn shop on that."

"That's the one."

"It's not you," I said, pausing for effect. "It's me they don't like."

Wendy burst out laughing. "Good," she said. "I was starting to worry. It usually takes at least an hour or two to dislike me that much."

"Do you think one of them followed you?"

"No, but I'll bet there was a lot of texting going on after I left."

"You're sure you didn't see anyone else?"

"See? Now you do think I'm some kind of nut."

I wished I could tell her what I actually was thinking: that one of those two bitchy old bats had decided to exert a little Sugar Maple brand of pressure on a non-magick visitor. I refused to even consider the appearance of the figure in the embroidered cloak. He was most likely one of our time-traveling stopover guests checking out the town despite the global request to steer clear of Sugar Maple until after the wedding.

Maybe I'd been too quick to blame the Souderbush boys for peeping through windows. The cloaked wonder was beginning to sound like a likely suspect.

"Don't worry," I said. "We'll get it all sorted out." I switched topics as gracefully as I could. "Can your stomach handle ibuprofen?"

"Like a champ."

I ducked into the store bathroom and shook two pills from the bottle then grabbed two bottles of water from the fridge near the back door.

"Take these," I said, handing Wendy one of the bottles. "They'll help."

.   .   .

SHE REACHED for the pills and her gaze landed on the stupid ring which, strangely enough, was no longer blinking. "That's an unusual engagement ring."

"You don't have to be polite," I said with a short laugh. "It's not my engagement ring." I gave her a brief history of how it came to be welded to my finger.

She popped the pills in her mouth then took a big gulp of water.

"So do you think we're really related?" I asked. No point beating around the bush.

"According to Bunny, we are. Apparently my father and your father were second cousins."

"And that makes us--?"

"Beats me," Wendy said, shaking her head. "I've never been good at the begats."

"Me neither." Then again, I never had to be. I studied her for a moment. "I don't really see a resemblance." She was younger, darker, and prettier without any help from magick.

She studied me back. "A little around the nose, maybe. I have my father's nose."

Maybe I did too but I'd never know for sure. There were no pictures of either of my parents. "Did your father ever talk about my father?"

"Not that I know of. He died when I was a baby."

"My dad died when I was six," I said. "I never got to hear his stories."

"That's the worst, isn't it?" Wendy's expressive face grew sad. "All of that personal history lost forever."

"I know everything about my mother." I was skating out onto thin ice but I couldn't seem to stop myself. "What I know about my father you could write on a matchbook cover and have room to spare."

"Same here. My mother never talked about him. She remarried when I was a toddler and it was like he'd never existed."

"What about the rest of the Aubrys?"

"There's a great uncle in Halifax, but he's very old. The last I heard, he was hanging on by a thread. That's about it. Family always meant my mother's blood relatives and my stepfather's clan."

"So it's just us," I said, kind of liking the word "us."

"Looks like it," Wendy said. "Unless there are some more out there waiting to get their DNA tested."

I wasn't sure if the idea filled me with joy or terror. All I knew was that I felt more comfortable, more quickly, with Wendy Aubry Lattimer than I had with any other human in my life. The connection had been immediate. The bond between us was powerful. Despite our obvious chemistry, it had taken a while for me to drop my guard around Luke. With Wendy, I felt like what remained of my guard was crumbling around my feet.

I unwrapped the ice bandage to give her skin a break from the extreme cold. The ankle didn't look great but at least the swelling hadn't gotten any worse.

"You're not going to be able to drive on this today."

"I'll bandage it up tight. I think I'll be fine."

She stood up, yelped, then sat back down again.

"I see what you mean," she said.

"I'll phone the Inn and have them send your bags to my place."

"I couldn't let you do that. If she has room for me, I can stay there for the night."

"I'm doing it," I said. "I walked to work this morning. We'll take your car to my place, okay?"

"The last thing you need today is to have a stranger on your hands."

"The last thing you needed was a sprained ankle."

"Good point," she said. "That means I'm in your debt."

"No, you're not," I said, patting her shoulder, "You're family."

Chapter 12

WENDY

I DON'T KNOW how Chloe managed it, but one hour later I was sitting at her kitchen table with my right foot resting on a wooden toy box with unicorns painted on it while four curious cats watched me from the doorway. The baby's nanny, Elspeth, had wrapped my ankle in cloths soaked in herbs and who knows what else and, combined with the ibuprofen, I was already feeling better.

"That's wonderful," I said as the Betty White clone bustled around the room. "Thank you!"

She grunted something I didn't understand and hurried off in a cloud of what I'd swear was essence of burned waffles.

"Don't mind Elspeth," Chloe said as she poured us each a tall glass of iced tea. "She's not big on the social graces but she's as loyal as they come."

"I really appreciate this," I said as I gratefully accepted the cold drink. "I don't know what I would have done without you."

"You would have figured something out," Chloe said, sitting down opposite me, "but I'm glad I was able to help."

"You don't have to babysit me," I said. "You're getting married tomorrow. There must be a million things you need to do."

"And I don't feel like doing any of them," she said, shaking her head. "I guess I wasn't born with the bride gene."

"Cold feet?" I asked. "That's not uncommon."

"Not cold feet," she said. "Just I already feel married to Luke and all of this craziness seems to be for everyone else."

"From what I heard, Bunny's loving every minute of it."

Chloe nodded. "That's part of the reason we didn't have a ceremony for just the two of us. It means so much to his mother."

"My ex's mother would have thrown a party if I'd changed my mind at the last minute."

Chloe looked at me, her golden eyes serious. "Is that why you divorced?"

I shrugged. "That and the supermodel replacement he had lined up."

"I'm sorry," she said, touching my hand. "That must have hurt."

"It still does," I acknowledged. "I was blindsided when he said he loved someone else."

"Do you still love him?"

I thought about that or a minute or two. "No," I said, to my surprise. "I'm not sure when I stopped, but I'm finally over him. Only my pride still hurts."

We talked a little about our romantic pasts. Mine was limited to Gary. Chloe's boasted a long line of single dates with non-starter candidates for happily-ever-after until the day Luke showed up in town to investigate the death of a politician's mistress.

"And that was it," she said. "I finally understood what that love-at-first-sight stuff was all about."

It had scared the hell out of her but in the end love conquered all.

"And then Luke decided to put down roots in Sugar Maple," I said.

"He's our chief of police," she said, not without a touch of pride. "And I'm *de facto* mayor. It's worked out pretty well for all three of us."

The baby. I had almost forgotten about the baby.

Even though I had my misgivings about the town, I could see where it would be a wonderful place to raise children.

"I'm dying to meet my—" I stopped. "Is Laria my cousin?"

"I don't know," Chloe said. "She'll be waking up pretty soon. She's not shy about asking for a diaper change at the top of her lungs. You may not want to claim kinship."

Maybe it was the ibuprofen, but my eyes filled with tears.

"Are you okay?" Chloe asked.

"Sorry. Babies are my Achilles heel." A fact I had hoped to keep to myself another decade or two. Not even my BFFs back home knew the depth of my longing for a child. I told her in as few words as possible about my inability to get pregnant and what it had done to my marriage. I thought I had done a pretty good job of keeping the emotional drama to a minimum but her eyes filled with answering tears when I finished, so maybe not.

My story wasn't a new one and it wasn't all that uncommon. Some women are luckier than others when it comes to the reproductive sweepstakes.

"There are a lot of options today," she said. "IVF. Surrogacy. Adoption."

"Or a fertile second wife," I said.

She gave my hand a quick squeeze. There really wasn't much else to say. We pretended intense interest in sipping iced tea and listening to birds chirping outside the kitchen window. For two virtual strangers, we had shared a fair bit of emotional baggage in record time and it was taking its toll.

We were probably both relieved when the back door swung open and a bubbly Bunny MacKenzie blew into the room with two of her daughters in tow and we were all rainbows and unicorns.

Bunny gave me a bear hug of epic proportions. She instantly sensed that Chloe and I had hit it off and was more than willing to take full credit for the situation.

Except for my ankle.

She switched quickly into nurse mode and after palpating my ankle and foot thoroughly, declared it was a minor sprain that would take care of itself. She even pulled a pair of crutches from the back of her minivan and propped them against the nightstand.

"Use them," she ordered. "Even if you're just getting up to use the bathroom."

I wasn't about to argue with the woman.

I liked Bunny. Her daughters were okay, if a little distant. Talk shifted to the impending nuptials and escalated swiftly to a fever pitch. Chloe seemed overwhelmed by the pre-wedding talk and accompanying chaos.

I knew exactly how she felt.

All I wanted to do was escape.

Somehow Chloe picked up on it and minutes later I was blissfully alone in her tiny guest room. Alone, of course, is a relative term. Her four house cats were watching me from their various perches but since they didn't want to talk about flowers, bouquets, boutonnieres, white carpets, bridesmaids, or cakes, I was fine with their company.

I considered texting my friends with an update but my thumbs weren't up to it. I leaned back against the flurry of pillows and closed my eyes. I wasn't a napper by nature, but the day had been long and stressful and surprisingly emotional. Sleep seemed like the only choice.

I was drifting off when I heard baby sounds from across the hall.

I burrowed deeper into the pillows.

The sounds grew louder, more insistent.

Chloe had live-in help but it didn't seem like Elspeth was doing much of anything to calm the baby.

Stay out of it, I told myself. The baby was fine. There was a houseful of real, live mothers on hand, including one who was a retired nurse. Unless the floors could use a good scrubbing, they didn't need my help.

But the baby didn't stop crying. She was crying for a reason. I knew at least that much about babies.

I swung my legs off the bed, ignored the crutches (sorry, Bunny!), and hopped my way across the hall to Laria's room.

I swung open the door and my heart seemed to stop. The crib was empty. The baby, clad in an adorable yellow-

and-white onesie, was across the room, trying to pull herself up by hanging onto a tall whitewashed dresser with moons and stars and planets painted on it.

A wobbly dresser that clearly wasn't attached to the wall.

I probably should have questioned why the baby was no longer crying but I was too worried about the dresser falling on her tiny body to follow that train of thought.

"Laria," I said, as calmly as possible. "Come here!"

The baby looked at me, wide-eyed and watchful.

"Don't tug at the dresser, honey. Why don't you come to me?"

Of course she didn't have a clue what I was saying. I was trying to divert her attention from trying to pull herself up by the unanchored dresser.

Unfortunately I wasn't half as interesting. She turned away from me and, babbling to herself, began to climb up the front of the furniture.

The dresser wobbled violently.

She grabbed for one of the drawer pulls and moved up higher.

The dresser swayed wildly.

What happened next is a blur. I remember hurtling myself toward Laria as the dresser tilted forward on two legs and the next thing I knew I was on the floor, cradling the baby with my body, while Elspeth pulled the dresser off my back.

Adrenaline flooded my body as she reached down and snatched the baby from me. I scrambled to my feet, oblivious to the ankle sprain.

"Where were you?" I shrieked. "She could have been killed!"

"The wee one is unharmed." She seemed totally unperturbed by the near-tragedy.

Relief almost dropped me to the floor. But I was still seriously pissed off. "What about me? That stupid dresser could have broken my back."

"No harm come to you, missy," she said, her bright blue eyes pinned on me like twin lasers. She was old as the hills and smelled like burnt waffles, but she had the gaze of a much younger woman. "You are as you were."

It wasn't until I was back in the guest room that I realized my sprained ankle was no longer sprained.

~

CHLOE

"WHAT IN HELL were you thinking, staging an accident?" I bellowed at Elspeth the second Luke's family left to get ready for dinner in Burlington. "You might as well have waved a magic wand while you were at it!"

"She is all she should be as kin," Elspeth said, totally unfazed by my outrage. "She rose to the challenge and protected the wee one as we would."

"You had no right to issue a challenge, Elspeth! Why would you risk exposing all of us that way?"

"I do what I need to do and nothing less."

"This isn't the seventeenth century!" I exploded. "We don't speak in riddles any longer."

"She is here among us, " Elspeth said with a remarkable degree of calm, "and here she will remain."

"Until after the wedding."

"Until the spirits wish otherwise."

"I think Wendy might have something to say about that."

"And she will," Elspeth said, "when the time to say it comes."

"Maybe it's time you went back to Salem," I said, shaking with anger. "I can't have you here compromising our safety."

"Watch and wait," she said, neither apologetic nor cowed. "When the trouble has come and gone, I will take my leave and not before."

"Great," I snapped, reluctant affection battling with white-hot anger. "I'll be counting the days."

Elspeth pulled one of her disappearing acts and I was left alone in the kitchen to try and figure out what in the name of everything magick I was going to tell Wendy when she asked what the ancient troll had been up to.

Except, of course, I couldn't tell Wendy that the butter yellow-haired Betty White clone was a troll. I couldn't tell any of the humans even a small part of the truth about Sugar Maple. I had expected the wedding weekend would be a tightrope walk but so far it was exceeding my worst nightmare.

And since when was Elspeth a fortuneteller? I don't recall ever seeing her bent over a crystal ball, gazing into the future. She was a troll. She had the abilities that came naturally to trolls, both Norwegian and other groups. But there was no doubt that she had issued a warning. *When the trouble has come and gone...* What trouble? When was it coming? Where was it going? Why did she have to speak in fortune cookie riddles?

"A few answers might be nice," I said to the empty kitchen.

Chapter 13

WENDY

CHLOE and I were sipping wine out on the back porch later that evening when her husband-to-be Luke came home from dinner with his family.

He was big and strong without being bulky, the classic tall, dark, and handsome hero authors wrote about. He was blessed with unusual dark green eyes that gave me the classic dead-eyed cop look when Chloe introduced us.

"So you two are related," he said, cracking open a beer and joining us on the top step.

"Second cousins a whole lot of times removed," Chloe said, gesturing toward him with her wine glass.

"You come by your detecting skills honestly, Luke," I said, switching the sleeping Laria to my left shoulder. "I don't know how Bunny put the clues together, but we're definitely family."

He nodded but I had the distinct sense he was less than happy that I was there.

"We'd always heard that Chloe didn't have anyone." His tone was even and non-threatening but there was something darker behind his words. "Funny that you'd turn up now."

I felt prickles of anger scratching up my spine. "Funny that your mother would ask me to."

Chloe leaned forward and put a soothing hand on his knee. "Actually Wendy was about to turn around and head back home when she hurt her ankle."

Luke's eyes went immediately to my ankles.

"It was my right ankle," I said icily. "And it feels a whole lot better now."

He nodded again but said nothing. Poor Chloe looked embarrassed and annoyed.

"We see a family resemblance," she said with mock cheer that fooled no one. "We both have our fathers' noses."

"Better than DNA," he mumbled into his beer.

I was very glad I wasn't the one marrying him day after tomorrow. The cop thing must be an acquired taste.

"How's this for a segue: since we're talking about fathers, I have something for you, Chloe." I ducked back into the cottage for my purse.

Luke wasn't smiling but at least he didn't look like he was about to arrest me when I handed Chloe the envelope.

"I'm sure you have tons of photos," I said, "but I had copies of this one made just in case it's not in your family album."

Chloe and Luke exchanged glances. What those glances meant was anyone's guess.

I noticed that Chloe's hands shook as she opened the envelope. Pre-wedding jitters maybe? Too much caffeine?

She reached inside and pulled out the shiny color snap-shot and, to my surprise, she started to cry.

The photo was your average, run-of-the-mill buddy picture. Chloe's father Ted was about twenty; my dad closer to thirty. They were both in jeans and t-shirts, arms draped across each other's shoulders. They were young and healthy, aiming big smiles toward the camera because life was going to last forever and this was just the beginning.

Luke stared down at the photograph, then put his arm around Chloe. She leaned into him, burying her face against his side and sobbed as if her heart were breaking.

Luke looked over at me and for the first time I could see the man Chloe had fallen in love with.

"This is Chloe's only photo of her father," he said, his voice cracking slightly. "You don't know how much this means."

He was right about that.

This was America, where your every move was caught on camera from first breath to last. Our fathers were both baby boomers, probably the most photographed generation up until that time. Christenings. Communions. First day of school. Proms and engagement parties, bridal showers and bachelor parties and sunny days at the beach. Instamatics. Polaroids. Disposable cameras. How was it possible that this was the only photo in existence of her father?

I watched quietly while the emotions played themselves out. I knew I should go back into the cottage and give them some privacy but I didn't want to miss a thing. I had grown up on a diet of Kinsey Milhone, Spenser, and reruns of *Murder, She Wrote*. I knew a good mystery when I saw one.

To be honest, a lot of things hadn't made sense since I arrived in Sugar Maple. The weird feeling that I was being talked about in Fully Caffeinated even though nobody said a word. The feeling I was being watched as I walked down the street. And what about the cloaked man in front of Sticks & Strings? Explain that one, if you can.

The only explanations I could come up with bordered on the insane. I glanced down at my right ankle. My perfectly healthy, unswollen, and unsprained right ankle. I mean, what was going on with that? Ibuprofen and ice can work wonders but they can't undo the damage. But moments after the drama with Laria and Elspeth, my ankle was good as new.

"You are as you were," Elspeth had said.

She was wrong.

I wasn't sure I would ever be the same again.

CHLOE

AT SOME POINT Wendy slipped back into the cottage for the night, leaving Luke and me alone on the front porch. The baby was asleep in her room, the sound of her breathing drifted through the baby monitor on the railing.

"I think she suspects something," Luke said as I finally slipped the precious photo of my dad back into the envelope.

"I know," I agreed and brought him up to speed on her adventures in Sugar Maple. "We used to be a lot better at keeping our secrets secret."

"I thought Meghan would be the first one to figure it out." His sister, after all, had had a very close encounter with a seductive Fae male that almost had tragic consequences.

"Wendy hasn't figured it out yet," I reminded him. "Mostly she just finds Sugar Maple weird."

He grinned at me. "I don't know how to break it to you—"

"Not funny," I said.

"You know I love it here." He crossed the porch to where I was sitting on the top step and sat down next to me. "It's my home now too."

"Something's going on," I said, lacing my fingers with his. "I can't pinpoint what exactly but I can feel it in my bones."

"That peeping tom thing."

"That's one."

"I thought we decided it was the Souderbush boys."

"I would've bet the yarn shop on it until what happened to Wendy."

"You want to run that by me again. I kind of got lost when she whipped out that picture of your dad."

I repeated Wendy's story about the now-you-see-him-now-you-don't figure lurking by the shop window.

"Sounds like something slipped through the barriers you set up."

"It's more than that," I said. "I've seen him too."

I could feel the tension as he gripped my hand a little tighter. "Where?"

"Through the Book of Spells." I described him down to the cloak embroidered with Dewi, Y Ddraig Goch, the Red Dragon of Cadwallader, in fiery reds and oranges.

"Sounds like the same guy," Luke said, clearly not thrilled by the revelation.

"He's not one of us," I said. "Who is he? Where did he come from? Why is he here now of all times?"

"Maybe he didn't get the memo," Luke said with a shrug. "We both know this town is like Grand Central Station for ghosts."

"They prefer to be called spirits."

"Whatever. Renate did a great job shutting down the flow of traffic, but a few stragglers were bound to slip through."

I leaned my head against his very solid, very human shoulder. "I hate it when you make sense."

"Forty-eight hours from now this will all be over," he said, holding me close. "The MacKenzies will be back in Massachusetts where they belong. Wendy will go home to Maine." He paused and brushed his lips against my temple. "And we'll finally be alone."

"Except for Laria," I reminded him.

"And Elspeth," he said.

"About Elspeth," I said. "Let me tell you what happened this afternoon…."

Chapter 14

GAVAN

That same evening

GAVAN HAD RECOGNIZED the troll at once: Elspeth, wife to Jacob, mother to many, devoted protector of Aerynn's mate Samuel until he pierced the veil. To see her living among mortals, caring for their young, being treated as family, surprised him.

If Elspeth, one of the great warriors of legend, found reason to protect the humans, maybe some of them could be trusted after all.

He had watched the drama from the limb of an old maple tree as the ancient troll baited the trap for the unsuspecting mortal female who called herself Wendy. And, he had found it hard to believe when the mortal risked her own safety to keep the tiny magick from harm.

Not that the dark-haired human knew the wee one

possessed powers. She was kin to Chloe along the human bloodline and possessed no magick of her own. The town's secrets were shrouded in spells and charms designed to mask their true nature from mortals. Still, her selfless act of bravery had moved him deeply. Far more deeply than he would have imagined possible.

She slept now, stretched across the narrow bed while four familiars kept watch over her. She wore the faded lower garment called jeans and a white top without arm covers. He reminded himself that humans were warm-blooded, prone to wild swings of body temperature that caused them to add and remove articles of clothing as comfort dictated. Her breathing was even and regular, her breasts rising and falling in a steady rhythm.

Humans required long, unbroken hours of sleep on a daily basis. Their bodies and minds were fragile engines that needed copious amounts of food, drink, and rest in order to work at their ultimate capacity.

He had much to do in the remaining day before the wedding. He needed to discover how far Chloe's human mate would go to protect the half-mortal, half-sorceress female. Rohesia had not known about the child when his mission began. A child who might one day be the most powerful of them all, despite the wide strain of human blood that ran through her tiny veins. It was a complication none had foreseen and needed careful consideration. Most parents, mortal and magick, would fight to the death to protect their offspring from harm.

He knew he should be digging deeper into Chloe's situation, devising a plan that would ensure the safety of his kind, but for reasons beyond his ken, he could not leave the sleeping human they called Wendy.

He had long heard about the treacherous human heart, the way it could shift from warm to icy cold in the blink of an eye. It was said that betrayal lay at its beating core. That might have been true once but all worlds, all dimensions had known change. Why should the realm of humans be different? He was descended from fierce soldiers who had fought for their right to survive in a violent and dangerous world, so unlike the world he had been born into.

This woman was different in ways he still didn't understand, ways that called to his deepest soul. Maybe it was the kindness she had shown to Chloe's child or the deep river of sadness he somehow sensed ran through her.

Maybe it was the feeling that together they would accomplish far more than they ever could accomplish separately.

Dangerous thoughts. He forced them from his mind. He was not here to find a new path for himself. He was here to follow a path chosen for him long ago.

The human called Wendy stretched slightly and curved her arm around the pillow. One of the familiars, a sleek black feline, met his eyes with a look that was equal parts dismissive and amused.

This was the woman he had observed in front of Chloe's knit shop.

He hadn't meant to cause her harm and he was grateful to the legendary warrior troll for bringing her healing skills to bear against Wendy's human pain.

The action had angered Chloe because it risked exposing Sugar Maple's true nature to the world, but he stood with Elspeth in this. To see a warrior troll risk a leader's wrath to reward a mortal was stuff of legend and

Rohesia had been deeply enraged when he communicated the news.

"The time is now!" she roared. "You will stop her wedding to the human and take his place."

He and Chloe would be wed, but he knew he would never take the mortal's place.

It didn't matter.

All that mattered was that the time for the promise to be fulfilled was within reach.

Chapter 15

CHLOE

The day before the wedding

MY ORIGINAL PLAN was to spend the day alone knitting the cobweb lace shawl I'd designed for my wedding to Luke. I was three-quarters of the way finished with the knitted-on edging and not entirely certain I would make it through both that and the fiddly, eight-hundred-stitch bind-off without losing my mind.

I knew I could always call upon magick to finish it in the blink of an eye but my knitter's soul would never be happy if I took the easy way. This was a labor of love and, like all labors of love, that meant no shortcuts.

Finished or not, I intended to wear it proudly but I'd definitely be happier if I didn't have a sixty-inch Addi Lace circular trailing behind me.

I'd been working on this in secret for the last few

months. Not an easy task when you run a yarn shop, live with a nosy cop, have an eight-month-old baby girl, and friends who can walk through walls without even trying.

So I had wielded my power as a bride-to-be and declared today off-limits to everyone but Luke and Laria and even they were banished until dinnertime.

I had all the yarn I needed. Extra double-points at my disposal. Good lighting. Lots of iced tea at the ready. The a/c was working full blast. The cats had sworn to mind their own business.

And, to my surprise, I asked Wendy to spend the day with me.

She had been halfway out the door, right on Luke's and Laria's heels, when I stopped her.

"I could use some help," I said, gesturing toward the pile of pre-wedding knitting tasks I had lined up. "If you wouldn't mind being put to work…"

Unless she was the world's best actress, she seemed to love the idea. "Don't laugh, but I love weaving in ends."

I rolled my eyes. "If I'd known, I would have saved a few mitered-square blankets for you."

She grinned back at me. "My idea of heaven."

We made a great team. She quickly finished the last inch of knitting on Laria's wedding outfit, completed the I-cord bind-off, and put it in for a good soak before blocking it to size.

"You're good," I commented. "Did your mom teach you how to knit?"

"YouTube and Ravelry," she said with a laugh. "Nobody in my family is very crafty."

"My mother was a brilliant knitter. She's the one who opened Sticks & Strings."

"And she taught you how?"

"I think so."

"You think so?" She looked puzzled. "You don't remember?"

"I was so young when she died, Wendy." I was aiming for casual candor. "What I really can't remember is a time when I didn't knit."

She nodded in agreement. "I know exactly what you mean. I was a senior in high school when I learned. I wish I'd started earlier." She snipped a few ends with quick, practiced clips of the tiny embroidery scissors. "Think of how many eight-foot garter stitch scarves I could have churned out."

"All hail, the humble garter stitch scarf," I said, carefully completing a double decrease after two yarnovers. "The shop owner's dream." In case you didn't know, garter stitch gobbles up the yarn like a hungry army of moths.

We were quiet while I maneuvered my way around a particularly tricky corner of the cobweb lace shawl. Clearly Wendy did a lot of knitting with friends. She understood when to talk and when to be quiet, the two most important attributes for a knitting circle member.

"So where did you grow up?" she asked as I paused to take a long sip of iced tea.

"Right here." I told her about Lilith's mother, Sorcha, and how I had been lucky enough to have an entire village guiding me toward adulthood.

"So Sorcha adopted you."

"Not legally, no."

She thought about that for a moment. "And nobody from the Aubry side showed up to see how you were getting on?"

"Not that I know of."

Once again I had skated out on very thin ice. There were no ready explanations for my upbringing that would make sense to a curious human.

Finally she spoke. "They didn't care that much about me either," she said, a hint of bitterness behind her words. "I think I saw my paternal grandparents once and I'm not even sure about that."

"Not every family is close," I said carefully.

"Tell me about it."

I knew what was coming next and I cast about frantically for an explanation a sane person would believe. I braced myself for the inevitable.

Wendy didn't disappoint. "How about your mother's side? They were originally from here, weren't they?"

The acronym K.I.S.S. danced before my eyes. *Keep It Simple, Stupid.* This might be the time to heed that advice.

"She was an only child," I said. "And her parents were already gone."

We refocused our attention on our knitting while unasked questions bounced around between us. Good thing, because I was pretty sure they were colliding with the answers I couldn't come up with.

I wanted desperately to ask her what she was thinking but I didn't dare. She was already suspicious of Sugar Maple and its inhabitants. Add my paper-thin family history and her warning bells must have been going off like crazy.

I had already volunteered more information than any sane sorceress would have. I was beginning to wonder if I needed to cast some kind of spell on myself that would help me keep my big, fat mouth shut.

Working an intricate lace edging on a humongous

cobweb lace shawl takes concentration and time. I was so close to actually finishing the job that I could taste it. There was even a chance I could block and dry it by the wedding tomorrow. It was hot outside, sunny, and with little humidity.

The odds were definitely in my favor.

Wendy disappeared into the laundry room to soak Laria's wedding outfit. Most people thought the baby should be garbed in white or ivory but I had opted for summery colors that made me smile. Wendy was in total agreement, which endeared her to me even more.

"Okay," she said a few minutes later. "I blocked the bolero and it's lying flat on the picnic table outside."

"I wish you lived closer," I said. (Seriously, where was the spell that would help me think before I spoke?)

"Me too." She fixed her big, dark brown eyes on me. "But just not in Sugar Maple."

"Excuse me?"

She started to laugh. "No, no! I don't mean you don't want me in Sugar Maple. I meant—no offense, Chloe—that I'm not sure I could live in Sugar Maple."

"What's wrong with Sugar Maple?"

Stupid question, Chloe! There goes that big mouth of yours again. You know darned well what's wrong with Sugar Maple.

"Come on," she said. "You must know there's a strange vibe going on here."

"What do you mean, strange vibe?" Who knew I was so good at playing dumb?

She fiddled with her iced tea spoon. "That what you see isn't all there is."

I forced a laugh. "Isn't that true of just about everywhere?"

"Not like this. I don't believe in ghosts, but if I did, I'd say this was a very popular spot."

Okay, now I was freaking out for real. She didn't have magick, I was sure of that, but she had something even more dangerous to Sugar Maple: smarts and curiosity.

And here I'd thought Bunny MacKenzie was the one I had to watch out for. When it came to adding up clues, my cousin Wendy could run rings around her.

I was deeply grateful when my cell phone vibrated and I excused myself to field a work call.

"We found a wicked good new indie dyer in western New York State," I said after I ended the call. "She has a technique that enables merino to soak up the color as if it were silk."

Wendy asked a few questions which I probably answered with way too much information. When it comes to knitting, I'm like the engineer who tells you how to make a watch when all you wanted was the time.

"Have you ever tried dyeing your own blanks?" I asked as I put down my knitting for a moment to give my hands a break.

She shook her head. "Too messy. I clean houses for a living. I want to keep my own place as trouble-free as possible."

I asked her how she got started cleaning houses and she ended up telling me about her failed marriage to Gary Lattimer. My eyes filled with tears more than once and I hoped she didn't notice. That's why I read romances: because life doesn't often come up with a happily-ever-after ending.

"And you really didn't see it coming?" I asked as she paused to sip some more iced tea. "Not even a clue?"

"I thought we were happy," she said with a bewildered shake of her head. "We never had one of those fiery, passionate marriages but we were solid." She stopped for a beat. "At least I thought we were solid."

Wendy had wanted a partner, someone to share the ins and outs of daily life. Someone to grow old with. A father for the children she had wanted so badly. She hadn't been looking for the sparks and fireworks kind of love that I had longed for.

"Did you love him?" So far, that was the one thing she hadn't mentioned.

Her eyes met mine. "I married him. I'd still be married to him today if he hadn't fallen in love with Sophie."

"But did you love him?"

"Of course I did."

"Really?"

"Okay," she said, "maybe not the same way you love Luke, but I did love Gary."

"Meaning what?"

"You're doing it again," she said, deflecting my question. "You sound like a prosecuting attorney."

I didn't back down. "You're the one who said it. I'm just trying to figure out what you meant."

"I was very young," she said. "I was flattered that he saw something in me. I figured the chemistry thing would work itself out."

"Did it?"

"Sure it did." She fiddled with her glass of iced tea. "With Sophie."

"Do you miss him?"

"Funny thing," she said. "I thought I did. I thought I missed everything about him, but it turns out that what I miss most is being married. I liked knowing I was in this life with someone who had my back." She forced a smile. "Even if it didn't last very long."

"Even if you didn't have any chemistry together?"

"I might rethink that part of the equation next time." A twinkle appeared in her eyes. "A few sparks might be nice."

I thought about the sparks that had literally leaped between us the first time Luke's hand touched mine. The sparks that still sprang to life when we were together. I wouldn't have missed that for the world. I wanted Wendy to know she didn't have to settle but I was afraid I'd already said far too much.

"I'm not usually this pushy," I said, picking up my knitting again.

"You're not pushy," Wendy said. "You're opinionated."

"Which is a nice way of saying I'm being a pain in the butt."

"Borderline," she said, "but you're not quite there yet."

"Good to know," I said. "I'm so accustomed to Bunny and company and their frontal assault on my privacy that I've lost all sense of personal boundaries."

"This was nothing," Wendy said. "You should hear my friends when we get together."

She made me laugh out loud with her stories about Diandra, Kelly, and Claire and their determined pursuit of a man for Wendy.

Then I made her laugh with stories about Janice and Lynette and the rest of Sugar Maple and their misbegotten attempts at matchmaking pre-Luke.

"And you guys met when he came to town to investigate a murder?"

I nodded. "One thing led to another and he decided to

take the chief of police job and make Sugar Maple his home."

"For love."

I couldn't deny it. "Yes," I said, feeling blessed. "For love."

~

WENDY

CHLOE and I took a lunch break around eleven-thirty. In what Chloe said was a rare gesture, Elspeth had put together a platter of tuna salad sandwiches and prepared another pitcher of iced tea for us.

"She must want something," Chloe mumbled good-naturedly as we carried them out to the back porch.

"Where is she?" I asked as we settled down on the rickety lawn chairs. "I haven't seen her at all today."

Chloe shrugged. "Laria is with Luke and his family. Elspeth has the day off."

We ate in companionable silence for a while then compared notes on what had yet to be done.

The baby's outfit was blocked and dried and ready to be unpinned from the towels.

"She's going to look adorable," I said, gesturing toward the yellow, green, and cream wonder.

"Thanks." Chloe grinned. "I think so too."

The shawl was another matter. She still had yards to go, and I wasn't convinced she'd be able to get to the finish line in time.

"I'll get it done," she said with grim determination. "I'll stay up all night if I have to."

"On the night before your wedding?"

"I'm still breastfeeding," she reminded me. "I haven't slept through the night since Laria was born."

"How about I take over when you need a break?"

She hesitated. I recognized the look. I'm one of those I-can-do-it-myself types too.

"I'd love to knit a few good thoughts in there for you."

"That would be great," she said, a big smile wreathing her face. "You've worked lace before?"

"I'm not in your class," I said, "but I've been watching you and I think I can do it."

"If you could handle the bind-off—"

"Done," I said. "Jeny's stretchy bind-off?"

"Perfect!"

We were discussing the merits of Jeny's stretchy bind-off versus Judy's magic cast-on when it happened.

A piercing whistle split the summer air. One loud, sharp note followed by two more in quick succession. We looked at each other.

"A bird?" I asked, not sure I wanted to see the bird that could make that sound.

Chloe went still. Her cell phone announced a text message but she ignored it.

Another whistle, longer and louder this time, and clearly coming from a point very close to where we were sitting.

"The roof," I said. "I'll bet there's a bird on your roof."

Chloe went freakishly pale and a moment later I found out why.

It wasn't a bird whistling on her roof.

It was her baby daughter.

Chapter 16

WENDY

"WE NEED A LADDER," I said, springing into action. "You keep her occupied while I—"

"No." Chloe's voice was unnaturally calm. "I'll take care of this."

A horrible thought crossed my mind. "You're not going to try to catch her when she falls, are you?"

"Wendy, you'll have to trust me on this. Laria is in no danger."

The top of my head almost exploded. "She's on the roof!" I yelled at the top of my lungs. "Your baby is on the roof!"

The look in Chloe's eyes stopped me cold. I saw compassion, acceptance, even shock, but I didn't see fear.

Her eight-month-old daughter was perched on her roof and Chloe wasn't scared?

"This is insane," I said. "You stand there and watch if you want, but I'm going to find a ladder and get that baby down."

She placed a hand on my forearm. "Trust me, Wendy." Her eyes fluttered closed for an instant "I'll explain everything later."

The only explanation I could come up with was that she was bat-crap crazy.

I was tempted to jump into my car and get the hell out of there as fast as humanly possible, but there was still a baby on the roof.

Or was there?

Chloe said something to Laria in a language I had never heard before. Laria stood up, seemed to consider her options, then suddenly rose up higher than the house.

I'm pretty sure I screamed. I mean, who wouldn't? But the scream was quickly replaced by a very real version of shock and awe.

Laria was flying.

I'd like to say she was just riding the thermals like a red-tailed hawk but that wasn't the case. She was in full control of where she went and how she got there. Her tiny face was alive with joy and excitement. She did loops and barrel rolls while her mother watched with a definite been-there-seen-that expression on her face.

And more than a touch of pride.

As for me, I was beginning to wonder if maybe I was the one who was bat-crap crazy because there was no way on this planet that this was really happening.

Except that it was.

I mean, I was awake. I'd consumed three cups of coffee and two glasses of iced tea. A dead person couldn't sleep, much less dream, after that much caffeine. I really was standing there in my distant cousin Chloe Hobbs's backyard in Sugar Maple, Vermont watching her baby daughter fly.

"Come here now, Laria!" Chloe had the universal don't-mess-with-mom tone down cold. After one last giggling loop around the house, Laria came in for a perfect landing in her mother's arms.

Chloe pressed a kiss to the baby's head then met my eyes.

"You probably have a few questions," she said.

"You have a flying baby," I said. "I just watched a baby fly."

Chloe pressed another kiss to Laria's head. "She has some . . . special skills."

"You think?" The kid could barely walk, but I had just seen her zoom around like Maverick in *Top Gun*.

Her cell phone announced another text. This time she glanced at her screen.

"It's Luke," she said with a bemused shake of her head. "Letting me know Laria is on her way home."

"Can he fly too?" It had to be asked.

"Of course not," she said. "He's only human."

"As opposed to what?" I asked her. "I mean, we're all—" I stopped mid-sentence. "We are, aren't we?"

Turns out, flying babies were just the beginning.

I listened for I don't know how long as Chloe outlined what was really going on in Sugar Maple.

My second cousin I-don't-know-how-many-times-removed was half-sorceress/half-human. Up until that moment, I didn't know it was possible to be half-human/half-anything. She said she had magical powers and after seeing her daughter perform maneuvers over the cottage, I wasn't about to argue the fact.

"You're saying that rosy-cheeked, bitchy little Midge Stallworth is a vampire?"

We were seated at the kitchen table. Laria, earthbound for the moment, was napping in her crib.

"Yes," Chloe said, "she's a vampire."

I was having trouble wrapping my human brain around it. "We're talking Dracula here, right? Lestat? The guy from *Dark Shadows?*"

"Times have changed. Modern technology eliminated the hunt."

Artificial blood on an auto-delivery program like Blue Apron. Who knew?

She must have noticed the look on my face and she grimaced. "'Hunt' might have been an unfortunate choice of words."

I started to laugh and then a second later Chloe joined in and before I knew it, we were cracking truly terrible vampire jokes that had us almost crying.

"I didn't know there were so many bad vampire jokes," she said, drying her eyes with a paper napkin.

"Neither did I." My stomach hurt from laughing.

"Did I tell you that Bunny says Midge creeps her out big time."

"Does Bunny know the truth?"

She shook her head. "Only you and Luke."

"You've managed to keep an entire townful of secrets from one of the nosiest women I've ever met?" I whistled. "Damn, you're good."

"It's taken spells, charms, magick, and a lot of prayers to Aerynn, but so far we've managed."

"Who's Aerynn?"

She gave me the *Reader's Digest* version of three hundred-plus years of family history, beginning with the Salem witch trials and ending at her kitchen table.

"I'm having trouble keeping up," I said, head spinning. "So all of the magick is on your mother's side."

"Don't worry. The Aubrys are one-hundred percent Homo sapiens, if that's what you're wondering."

To my surprise, I was a little disappointed.

Chloe told me that she had lived the first thirty years of her life raised by magickal beings in a magickal town without any magick of her own.

"Not even a few card tricks?"

"Everyone had pretty much written me off as the last in the line of Aerynn's descendants but then Luke came to town and everything changed."

"I thought Luke was human."

"He is," she said. "Falling in love was the key to my magick."

"How did the rest of Sugar Maple feel about that?"

She glanced away for a moment. "There are still some pockets of serious resentment."

"Like the owner of the Inn?"

"You have good instincts," she said. "Renate used to be one of my closest friends. We've been working at mending fences."

"So what is she?" I asked. "Another vampire? A werewolf?"

"She's Fae."

"As in fairy tales?"

She laughed. "Not even close."

I listened, struggling to keep my jaw from hitting the

kitchen table. She told me about Isadora and her two sons, Gunnar and Dane. About glitterprints and ancient grievances and battles to the death. (Or what passed for death in this Neverland I found myself in.) And the Weavers who ran the Sugar Maple Inn.

"You're telling me that Renate and her entire family are Fae who live under the windowsills in the Inn."

"They take human form when needed." She gave me a sheepish look. "Usually a very pleasing human form."

"So that's why everyone is so smoking hot around here." If you're going to take human form, why not be beautiful. It made sense to me.

"We may have overdone it a tad."

The Fae, however, were supernaturally gorgeous to a dangerous degree and they used it to their advantage.

"The Fae are your enemy?"

"Not always and not all Fae."

"I'm confused."

"So was I for a very long time. I'm still playing catch-up." She told me that the Fae had been at the heart of all Sugar Maple's troubles the last few years.

I let the info rattle around in my brain for a few moments. "Does this mean the guy in the fancy cloak is one of yours?"

"I wish it did," she said. "I don't have a clue who he is, but I've seen him too."

"By Sticks & Strings?"

She shook her head. "A few days ago, but in a different dimension."

The crazy-big ring on her slender hand suddenly began to glow brightly.

"So is that a magick engagement ring?"

She made a face. "You noticed the glow."

"You could land a 757 by the light that thing gives off."

She told me again about finding the ring in an old shoebox filled with mementoes. "I slipped the damn thing on to keep it away from the baby and the next thing I knew, it shrink-wrapped itself to my finger."

"So take it off."

She shot me a look. "If I could take it off, do you really think I'd still be wearing it?"

I reached out to touch the glowing metal but pulled back at the last moment. You didn't need magickal powers to feel the harnessed power in the room. I had never felt more vulnerable, or more human, in my life. "It looks like it's glowing in Morse code."

"I hate it!" She burst out, eyes filling with tears. "My Sugar Maple friends think the ring is casting some kind of spell over us. The MacKenzies can't stop asking questions. Bunny's ready to go at it with a pair of wire cutters and—" She met my eyes and in her gaze I saw both fear and sorrow. "I've felt it for weeks, Wendy. Change is in the air. I feel it in my bones."

"Wedding nerves," I said, trying desperately to make light of her fears. "It happens to every bride."

"This is more than wedding nerves," she persisted.

"Have you talked to Luke about it?"

She nodded. "He can't see what I see. The danger isn't from his world. It's from mine and there's nothing I can do to stop it."

Chapter 17

GAVAN

THE BETROTHAL RING on his hand blinked as he watched them through the kitchen window.

Humans, even half-humans, were unpredictable. Chloe had revealed Sugar Maple's secret to the mortal named Wendy and, to his deep surprise, the mortal seemed to accept it without fear or aggression.

Chloe was right when she said something terrible was coming. The life she loved was about to be torn apart by an old promise made by loving parents who didn't know they were hours away from leaving their child forever.

Guinevere and her mortal mate had wanted to ensure their young daughter's safety.

Rohesia had wanted to ensure their clan's future.

A simple promise, they had believed, one that would be easily kept.

He understood sacrifice. He had seen sacrifice in action over the course of his life. His clan's situation was dire. All that he knew, all that he loved, would cease to exist if he was unsuccessful. The path forward was clear and he was willing to hand over his future to secure a future for all.

Maybe Chloe of Guinevere would surprise him. She was half-human, but magick flowed through her veins, same as it flowed through his. She had chosen to live her life in Sugar Maple, raise her family side by side with those she had fought to protect. In any dimension, that meant something.

Maybe she would understand why it had to be this way.

It would be easier if she did, but ultimately it didn't matter.

Her fate had been decided a long time ago.

Chapter 18

CHLOE

Early evening

"WENDY KNOWS ABOUT SUGAR MAPLE?" Luke asked.

"You sound surprised," I said. "The baby dive-bombed her head. I think she figured it out for herself."

We were sitting on the living room sofa, eating take-out Chinese. Wendy was holed up in the guest room, working the bind-off on my wedding shawl. From the sounds of splashing and giggling drifting down the hallway, Laria was having her evening bath, courtesy of Elspeth.

"How much did you tell her?" he asked.

"Pretty much everything." No point denying it.

"You trust her?"

"Yes. Actually I do."

"How the hell can you trust someone you don't even know?"

"I trusted you," I reminded him, "and that's worked out pretty well."

His cop-face softened for an instant, just long enough for me to register the fact. "It took a hell of a lot longer than twenty-four hours."

"Apples and oranges," I said. "I was falling in love with you and I only had one chance to get it right." Being a descendant of Aerynn had a few downsides and that was one of them. Love came once to us and it was forever.

I told him that Wendy was family, part of the DNA I had inherited from my mortal father. I had never thought I would be lucky enough to know any of my father's kin and meeting Wendy was an unexpected and wonderful gift.

He put down his chopsticks and leaned back against the sofa. "I don't want you to be hurt."

"She wouldn't hurt me."

"You don't know that."

"I think I do."

"You're being naïve."

"You're being a cop."

"For all you know she's back there texting her friends."

"She's a knitter," I said, knowing how stupid that sounded to a non-knitting cop. "She's not going to be texting anybody until she finishes that eight-hundred-stitch bind-off."

"And then what happens?"

Sparks were starting to fly and not the good kind.

"I don't know," I said, jaw clenched.

"You don't trust my mother with the truth and you've known her a hell of a lot longer than you've known Wendy Aubry Lattimer."

"I love your mother, but she isn't my blood." Not to

mention the fact that Bunny MacKenzie was a world-class gossip and snoop.

"She cleans houses for a living," he persisted. "She can't be making a fortune. How do you know she won't make a few phone calls and sell the story for big bucks?"

"I don't," I said, my jaw clenched even harder.

"You told her to keep her mouth shut, didn't you?"

The relentless barrage of human logic made me want to scream. "I didn't think I had to." I tried to ignore just how ridiculous that statement sounded. "It was understood."

"Tell her."

The take-out cartons on the coffee table in front of us were starting to levitate from the force of my anger. "Don't push it, Luke."

"If you don't tell her to keep the secret, then I will."

The chopsticks began to spin around the room.

"This is none of your business."

"I'm your husband."

"Not yet."

"Okay, then I'm your lifetime partner," he went on. "I'm also Laria's father." He paused and gave me a bone-shaking dead-eyed cop stare. "And I'm the Sugar Maple chief of police. It's my job to keep this town safe and if that means telling your cousin to keep her mouth shut, then that's what I'm going to do."

As if on cue, the monster ring on my finger began doing its Morse code imitation.

"By the way," Luke said, "I hate that goddamn ring."

Finally something we could agree on.

∾

WENDY

THERE IS nothing like an eight-hundred-stitch bind-off to take a girl's mind off the fact that her cousin was a sorceress.

I mean, if someone asked you to define the word "sorceress," would you even know where to start?

How do you process the fact that your cousin had magickal powers? How do you absorb the fact that her baby daughter flew around the backyard like she had a jetpack in her onesie? How do you even begin to process the idea that the women sitting next to you at lunch in that very ordinary coffee shop were vampire and werewolf?

You don't.

You either accept it as a truth or you reject it and move on.

I accepted it, but that didn't mean I had absorbed it. Not even close. I wasn't sure I would live long enough to absorb everything Chloe shared with me. I suppose we all wonder at one time or another whether there was more going on in the world than we saw. We wonder about ghosts and devils, about heaven and hell. We hope in the deepest part of our hearts that we would meet up one day with our departed loved ones.

But we don't know for sure.

I knew for sure, however, that I had seen a human baby fly around the back yard under her own power.

Belief had to start somewhere.

Knitting has a way of giving you what you need when you need it. I wanted to empty my mind of everything but the project in front of me: hundreds and hundreds of cobweb lace stitches that needed to be bound off and emergency-blocked in time for Chloe's wedding tomorrow. There wasn't room in my addled human brain for anything else.

My smartphone had exploded with messages from Diandra, Kelly, and Claire, all demanding an update. I took a photo of the shawl I was working on and thumbed in a quick "Having great time. Wedding tomorrow. 800 stitches to go!!" and turned off the phone.

Normally I would have shared every last detail of my outrageously crazy day--flying babies, vampires, magickal spells and all. That's what best friends did. They told each other everything. I had shared the details of my divorce, and all the stages of grief that came with it.

But for some reason I drew the line today.

Chloe hadn't asked me to keep her secrets, but I knew that was because she trusted me to do exactly that. In record time, we had formed a bond that surprised both of us with its depth and its strength. I would never do anything to hurt her. I could only imagine the hell that would break loose if the world found out about Sugar Maple.

Besides, what sane person would believe me?

Which was why I was glad I had a lapful of fiddly knitting to keep me from thinking about anything beyond passing one stitch over the other. I had reached TMI hours ago. One more piece of information and I was sure my head would implode.

I was about a hundred stitches in when there was a knock on the door.

"Come in," I mumbled, a stitch marker gripped between my teeth.

The door opened. Luke stood there, his expression opaque.

"Got a minute?" he asked.

"Sure," I said, reluctantly laying down the knitting. "What's up?"

"Chloe told you about Sugar Maple."

The man didn't believe in beating around the bush.

"She didn't have to. Laria made the situation pretty clear."

His smile was gone before I could be sure I'd actually seen it. "That's exactly what Chloe said."

"I guess we're a lot alike."

"With one major exception."

I nodded. "I'll admit it's a big one."

He gestured toward the chair next to the window and I motioned for him to sit. He eased his long frame into it, looking a bit like a bull in a china shop. Assuming bulls sat down in china shops, that is.

"You probably have a lot of questions," he said.

I nodded.

"And I'm probably the only one who can answer them."

I took a long breath and then jumped into the deep end of the pool. "How long did it take you to believe it?"

His grin was equal parts rueful and amused. "I'm still not one hundred percent."

"I saw a baby fly." I met his eyes. "There really isn't any other possible explanation but the rational part of my brain keeps screaming, 'You're dreaming, Wendy! Wake up!'"

"Most people would be scared, faced with a situation like this." His inner cop was beginning to peek through.

"Were you?"

"Hell, yeah! Vampires, werewolves, all the things we were taught as kids didn't exist and here they are, right in front of your eyes. I'd never even heard of a selkie and now I'm good friends with one." He dragged a hand through his dark hair. "Nothing out there can prepare you for something like this."

"And yet you decided to build a life here."

"I didn't have a choice."

My eyes widened. "Are you saying she put a . . . spell on you?"

"She didn't have to. I fell in love."

"Did you ever ask her to renounce her powers?"

"This isn't an episode of *Bewitched*."

"And you weren't even tempted to ask?"

"Once or twice," he said with endearing candor, "but then she wouldn't be Chloe."

"How did you know it would work?"

"We didn't. I guess you could say we took a leap of faith."

"How have you managed to keep it from your family? Bunny isn't exactly the shy and retiring type."

"We've had a few close calls, but so far, so good." He said he knew that their luck would run out one day but until then their secret was safe. "You can't tell anyone about Sugar Maple, Wendy. Maybe Chloe didn't make that clear but I don't want there to be any mistake about that."

"Chloe knows she can trust me."

"That's great, but I don't trust anyone. I need your word."

"You have my word."

"I'm going to hold you to it.

"To keep Chloe and Laria safe?"

"To keep them *all* safe," he said.

～

I SAT on the edge of the bed after Luke left and stared out the window.

To keep them all *safe.*

His words kept spinning through my mind. Five simple words that told me everything about love and honor and commitment that was worth knowing. People climbed mountains looking for adventure. They went deep-sea diving. They bought tickets for space flights and flew hot-air balloons around the world in search of excitement. I wondered just how many of these wild and crazy risk-taking adrenaline junkies would have the guts to do what Luke had done: make a life here in Sugar Maple.

"I envy you," I said out loud. They had a home, friends, a precious baby daughter, and, most important of all, they had each other.

Maybe the secret to happily-ever-after included a touch of magick.

Chapter 19

GAVAN

The night before the wedding

THE MAN SAW HIM. Their gazes met in the glass wall between them and in that moment Gavan understood how much there was to learn about this new world before they could be part of it.

He didn't understand the properties that governed the glass walls they called windows. Twice they had revealed his presence through reflections much like those found in water, first to Wendy and now to the mortal known as Luke.

Rohesia had warned him to remain undetected but this new world tripped him up at every turn.

He willed himself away from the cottage, gliding deep into the woods where he felt more at home. A giant had laid claim long ago to the mountaintop where he spent his days in rumbling slumber so he settled on lower ground near the waterfall and portal. The waterfall of charged energies worked upon him as food and drink did upon humans. For the first time since leaving his home, he felt whole.

His Old World powers were unable to navigate easily through the web of both manufactured human energies and New World magick energies that shielded Sugar Maple. He had tried again to contact Rohesia, but he was met with a blaze of silver static that blocked communication. He could feel Rohesia's impatience building.

New World powers were unfamiliar to him. They were more complex, more adaptable to situations he had yet to discover. Were they stronger than the powers his people possessed or only different?

Chloe's human mate had displayed admirable qualities toward the magicks in his care. He saw no evidence of the atrocities inflicted on the unprotected during the dangerous years but clearly caution was still required.

The wedding was scheduled to take place tomorrow. When the time came, would his quest for survival prevail over their need to protect their own?

The future was unknowable.

All he could do now was wait.

Chapter 20

CHLOE

The morning of the wedding

"YOU WERE RIGHT," I said to Luke as I nursed Laria at sunrise. "I'm going to put a spell on Wendy. I don't know why I fought you over it." I hadn't worked out the details but I knew I needed to protect Sugar Maple from discovery.

"I'm not so sure I was right. I spoke to her last night while you were taking a shower," he said. "She understands what's involved. I think you can trust her."

"Since when is 'think' good enough?" He was a cop, after all. Cops liked absolutes.

"Gut instinct," he said with a shrug. "I believe her."

"People talk," I reminded him. "They don't always mean to, but sometimes things just pop out." My face reddened as I remembered the unfiltered way I'd spoken to

Wendy right from the start. If Laria hadn't spilled the beans, I wasn't entirely sure I wouldn't have.

"What kind of spell would you cast? Can you pick and choose like you're placing an order from Thai Palace?"

"That's the problem," I said. "I don't know and I don't have time to find out."

"This hasn't turned out to be the wedding week we were hoping for," he said, pouring me a big glass of orange juice.

I switched Laria from my right breast to my left. "Not even close."

"Next time we elope," he said.

"There won't be a next time," I said. "This is my one and only wedding."

His beautiful green eyes met mine and I found myself once again thanking the fates that we had found each other.

I hated when we argued. We are both strong-willed, highly-opinionated individuals and that meant we butted heads from time to time. We were on a steep learning curve when it came to first-time parenthood and when you added magick and matrimony to the mix, it was no wonder things got a little volatile now and then.

We fell silent, enjoying the moment for however long it lasted. Laria's nursing grew slower and her eyelids began to flutter shut. Wendy was still asleep in the guest room. Elspeth was doing whatever it was she did when I nursed. The MacKenzies were due to swoop down on us around nine a.m., when Janice and her glam squad would get us ready for the ceremony. This was probably the last bit of peace and quiet we would know for the rest of the day.

Lemony sunshine spilled through the open windows and traced patterns across the kitchen table. The raucous cries of blue jays, hungry for another handful of peanuts, made us smile.

"I saw someone at Wendy's window last night."

I was instantly on red alert. "The peeping tom?"

The cop face was back. "What peeping tom?"

"Oh crap." I felt like an idiot. "They were talking about him yesterday at the fitting. I guess I forgot to tell you."

"You're saying Sugar Maple has a peeping tom?"

"Bunny saw a face outside her window at the Inn. Isolda and Janice didn't see anyone, but they both had the feeling they were being watched."

I had also forgotten to tell him about the man in the embroidered cloak who had been peering into Sticks & Strings when Wendy approached. I made up for that omission now.

"I'd chalked it up to the Souderbush boys and eternal teenage boredom, but now I'm not so sure."

The Souderbush boys were lanky kids who would never grow past mid-puberty. They were nothing like the man Wendy had seen.

"This was definitely a big guy," Luke said.

"Human?"

"I doubt it. I could pretty much see right through him."

"I'm not sure if that makes me feel better or worse."

"Don't get me wrong," Luke said. "I'm not crazy about guys, dead or alive, peeking in our windows but I don't think it's anything to worry about." He said a few spirit stragglers had slipped through our barrier this week but with a little help from the locals, they had been located and turned away. "He was probably one of them."

It was as good an explanation as any. I pushed the vision of the guy from the Book of Spells from my mind.

Or at least I tried to.

The persistent feeling that trouble was on its way reared its head again but I was maxed out on worry. It would be nice to put everything on hold for a few hours and enjoy the fact that I was about to marry the love of my life. The peeping tom would have to wait.

WENDY

I DON'T THINK I slept more than an hour on the night before the wedding. Every time I closed my eyes, I saw Laria launching herself from the roof of Chloe and Luke's cottage and taking a solo flight around the backyard.

Try sleeping after that.

The cottage was bursting at the seams by the time I slipped into the kitchen for juice and coffee. I tried to stay out of the way but Chloe made sure I was drawn into the thick of things. I had a hard time remembering who was magick and who wasn't. The MacKenzie women mingled with the ladies of Sugar Maple and after awhile I found it didn't really matter.

Janice did something amazing to my hair with a flat iron and a little product, then handed me off to one of her assistants who transformed my bare face into something camera-ready.

Bunny buzzed around, looking spectacular in a pale green dress and summery hand-knit shawl.

"I'm so glad you're here," she said, giving me a warm hug.

"So am I," I said, hugging her back. "Thank you for making this happen."

I was in a place I never thought I would be, surrounded by people (both mortal and magick) I would never have met if Bunny MacKenzie hadn't set out to find me. The world would never look the same again. My eyes had been opened to possibilities I had never dreamed existed in our three-dimensional world and I was grateful.

When I was a kid, I had a recurring dream about a secret door that opened into an enormous sun-filled room that held another secret door that opened into yet another room and—well, you get the picture.

My old life in Bailey's Harbor seemed very far away.

~

GAVAN

HE WATCHED unseen as the mortals and magicks assembled for the ceremony. Two females of similar appearance and age hugged in an exuberant expression of affection between them and he was shocked to realize one was mortal and one was magick.

In fact, everywhere he looked, mortals and magicks were celebrating together.

Rohesia was wrong. Just the thought strengthened him. Sugar Maple was not a fortress that served to keep visiting and settled magicks safe from marauding humans. Instead, it was a peaceful settlement where both sides traded, mingled, and coexisted in harmony. A return to the fabled time when peace reigned in northern Wales, but better.

The reports of peace brought back from magicks upon their return from visiting the Spirit Trail were true. Despite his training and devotion to Rohesia, he knew he was right. He had seen the love and devotion that the half-magick Chloe and the human Luke had for each other. He had seen the deep respect the warrior troll, Elspeth, had for Chloe's chosen mate, Luke. And he had even felt an undeniable attraction to Chloe's human kin, Wendy.

He had also heard Chloe tell Wendy how her love for Luke had brought her powers to life and that Aerynn's line only loved once. Instinctively he knew that all the collective magick of his world could never make Chloe yield to him. The only way to bring the clans together was to join the celebration, not oppose it.

There would be no future for his clan in this dimension if that future was built on a foundation of bitterness and strife. If they were to find a place in the world of the new magicks, they would have to learn to embrace change or disappear forever.

He would not stop the wedding of Chloe and Luke. He would not break up a child's family.

And it was in that moment that he finally understood what he must do: Blueflame Rohesia immediately and tell her he would still do all in his power to facilitate the move to Sugar Maple, but the wedding would go forward.

∼

CHLOE
Proctor Park – early afternoon

. . .

THE HOUSE SPRITE team had transformed a portion of Proctor Park into a wedding wonderland. Somehow they had managed to make it look like a team of run-of-the-mill humans had been working for days to erect the tents, set up the tables and chairs, create the altar area from the old gazebo where Luke and I would exchange promises.

We couldn't have asked for better weather. Sunny, bright, not terribly hot or humid. The faintest hint of fall was in the air, hinting at what the next few weeks would bring.

And I still couldn't shake the feeling that this was all too good to be true.

The annoying ring had started blinking fast and furious the second we arrived at the park and showed no signs of stopping. Too bad we weren't having a winter wedding. A pair of heavy leather gloves would have helped block the light.

Luke had asked Janice's husband Lorcan to stand up for him while Janice had happily agreed to be my matron of honor. I had originally intended to walk down the aisle with Laria in my arms but asking Wendy to do the honors seemed the right and natural thing to do. Elspeth was delighted to hold the baby who looked beyond adorable in her new outfit.

"You look beautiful, honey," Bunny said, giving my arm a squeeze. "That wrap is exquisite."

I told her Wendy had executed the fiddly bind-off for me, which elicited more exclamations of approval.

"Thank you," I whispered in Bunny's ear. "I'm so glad she's in my life."

"I'm glad too," she said, giving me a full-on hug.

Everyone who was important to us was there that afternoon, including some unexpected guests. Manny, Frank, and Rose from Sugar Maple Assisted Living had decorated their motorized wheelchairs with huge white hydrangea blooms. Midge Stallworth and her husband held sunblocking parasols over their heads. I had the feeling it was more about nosiness than friendship but still they had joined us just the same.

Fran Kelly, Luke's old friend from his days with the Boston P.D., and her husband were there, front and center, to share our big day. I could see that Luke was deeply touched by their gesture.

Of course, all of the MacKenzies were there to celebrate the occasion.

"Showtime!" Janice called out. "Places, everyone!"

The MacKenzie women blew kisses in my direction then hurried up front to take their seats.

A billowy white cloud drifted over the gazebo and floated away.

"Please don't rain!" I muttered. "That's all we need."

"It wouldn't dare," Lynette said with a fierce scowl. "I won't let it!"

And, knowing Lynette, she meant it.

I suddenly found myself deeply grateful to be able to share this amazing day with both dear friends and new family.

"Suck it up!" Janice ordered. "This isn't a Hallmark movie, Hobbs. Your mascara's not waterproof so blink back those tears."

She winked and I couldn't help but laugh.

"It's really happening," I said, my gaze moving from Janice to Lynette to Wendy. "Luke and I are getting married."

I didn't think it would make a difference in how I felt but the idea of taking those ancient vows in front of everyone we loved was profoundly—and unexpectedly—moving.

"I wish—" I stopped, unable to say the words.

"I know," Lynette said, her eyes suspiciously damp. "Me too."

If only Gunnar could be there too. My childhood friend's sacrifice had made my future possible. Luke and I owed him one and I prayed one day we would be able to thank him.

Janice gave my hair a quick touch-up. Lynette fussed with my dress. Elspeth held Laria up for inspection and a kiss.

Wendy took her place next to me. "Ready?"

I nodded. "Ready."

We linked arms and waited as Elspeth and Laria took their seats up front. Janice and Lynette did the bridal walk to the makeshift altar to harp accompaniment courtesy of Bettina Weaver Leonides.

Wendy and I stepped onto the white carpet to a chorus of appreciative sounds from the assembled guests but only Luke mattered.

I was vaguely aware of Lorcan and Luke's brother Ronnie standing next to him, big smiles on their faces, and of Janice and Lynette on the other side, beaming at me.

Wendy murmured something in my ear then put my hand in Luke's.

Lynette's husband Cyrus, an internet-ordained minister, stepped forward and began to speak.

"We are gathered here together today to celebrate the marriage of our beloved Chloe and her partner Luke."

Cyrus's voice rang out with the practiced ease of the trained actor he was.

The words were more magical than any of our spells. They spoke to the essence of love and my heart soared with every second that brought us closer to declaring our eternal bond.

Finally it was time.

"I, Luke, choose you, Chloe, to be my wife, my partner, my soulmate in good times and bad, in health and in sickness, for now and forever."

Tears streamed down my face as I struggled to pull myself together. "I, Chloe, choose you, Luke, to be —"

And then it all came crashing down.

Chapter 21

CHLOE

THE WORLD WENT dark and silent. Next to me Luke was statue-still, his hand rigid in mine.

Someone or something had cast a freeze-spell on us.

"Chloe!" Wendy's whisper floated toward me. "What's going on?"

"I don't know," I whispered back. "See if you can get to Laria while I figure out what's happening."

If both Wendy and I were untouched by the spell, odds were good that Laria was untouched as well.

I sensed rather than saw a large male form looming behind me. I took my shaking hand from Luke's rigid one and quickly turned around.

"Show yourself!" I demanded.

And he did: by the glowing light of a ring that was the twin of the one that had been welded to my hand for weeks.

He was drop-dead gorgeous so he had to be Fae. But he wasn't one of our own. He was the man I had seen in the Book of Spells, the one who had walked through the fire toward me.

"I am called Gavan of Eres," he said, "and I am not here to hurt you or yours."

I'd heard that one before, usually seconds before one of my enemies launched a lightning bolt in my direction.

"Did you do this?" I asked.

"No."

"You didn't turn everyone into statues?"

"No," he said again. "It was—"

Before Gavan of Eres had the chance to finish his sentence, a heavy metal chain dropped from the sky and snaked its way around him, rendering him as immobile as the rest of the wedding party. A little old school for my taste, but effective. Whoever I was dealing with operated from a different playbook. I wondered who would have the advantage.

Laria whimpered and my breasts began to fill with milk. I had to trust that Wendy would keep her safe while I tried to determine what exactly I was dealing with. Not an easy thing to do when everything in me wanted to tear the world apart to find my child.

"Cat got your tongue?" I asked my captive friend. His attention was clearly elsewhere, which angered me even more than the let's-turn-out-the-lights parlor trick. He was staring up at the darkness as if he expected skywriting. "What's going on? Who's doing this?" I'd get to the *why* later.

"I am." The voice was female, strong and authoritative, and it surrounded us like fog.

"I'm tired of tricks," I snapped, more scared than angry but nobody had to know that but me. "Undo your mischief or I have nothing to say to you." I knew that no magick worth her salt wanted her best spells referred to as mischief. I was bound to get a reaction but apparently she didn't get the memo.

"Silence, Chloe of Guinevere."

Chloe of Guinevere? Had we time-traveled back a few centuries when I wasn't looking?

I wasn't about to stay silent. Not when my baby was somewhere in the darkness and the man I loved was a department store mannequin.

"You have ten seconds to tell me what's going on before I drag you down here and make you tell me." It sounded good if you didn't consider the fact that I still had no idea who or what was behind the commanding voice. Or if it even had a body I could drag anywhere.

Next to me, the man named Gavan said something. I moved closer to catch his words and my hand brushed against his and just like that my ring came back to life and so did the sun.

The sudden explosion of light was startling. My eyes struggled to adjust to the transition from utter darkness. I saw Wendy standing about thirty feet away with Laria in her arms. It took Laria a nanosecond to break free and float straight for me.

The feel of her in my arms, the sense of relief I felt knowing she was safe, took me out of the zone. I was shocked to realize that the image of a woman in fiery orange and red robes now filled the sky above the gazebo.

At least now I knew who I was dealing with.

"Oh my god," I heard Wendy say as she joined Laria and me. "She's beautiful!"

Of course she was. She was clearly Fae.

Which meant she could be dangerous.

"Five more seconds," I said to the giant image as I held my daughter close. "Restore us to what we were and then we'll talk."

"The time to talk is over. You will honor the commitment and join our clans together before the next sunrise."

Definitely old school.

"What commitment? I don't know what you're talking about."

Showers of hot glitter, carnelian red and silver, spilled over us. I shielded the baby from them as best I could.

"Chloe of Guinevere knows nothing of the betrothal." It wasn't easy to sound tough when you were bound in chains but Gavan managed. "She has chosen her mate, Rohesia. They have created a child together. We must find another way."

I was having trouble processing the fact that Rohesia of legend had stepped out of the Book of Spells and into my life.

The Old Magicks had divided into three groups during the early persecutions in what would one day be northern Europe. The clan that produced Aerynn had risked all to migrate across the ocean to what they hoped would be a more tolerant home among mortals. Bronwyn and her followers, unable to accept change, pierced the veil forever while it was said that Rohesia ultimately took her family of Others beyond the mist.

But here she was, looming over me, demanding I honor

a commitment I was hearing about for the first time. This wasn't how we did things here. At least, not in this century.

"The rings bind you together and have ever since Guinevere and I struck the bargain between us."

"I still don't know what you're talking about."

Gavan spoke up again. "Our families betrothed us to each other when we were children. Your mother wanted to ensure your safety if something should happen to her or to your father. Rohesia wanted to ensure asylum for our clan when the time came."

"Silence!" Rohesia ordered. "I will say all that needs to be said."

"No." He made that one simple word carry a multitude of meanings. "It is time for you to listen before there is no time at all."

I have to admit the man had a way with words. I glanced quickly at Wendy. My cousin was utterly transfixed. Her fear had been replaced with what seemed to be a sense of wonder.

"It was I who gave you that ring," Rohesia said to me.

"I found this ring in a cardboard box."

"That ring was put in your parents' care until the proper time."

"My parents are dead," I said flatly. "They died when I was six."

Suddenly I understood. Bits and pieces of long-buried memories floated to the surface. A beautiful woman. A young man. My mother's tears. My father's reluctance. A ring that would one day be mine. We had been on n the way home from meeting with Rohesia about my future when the accident took my parents' lives.

Rohesia was watching me closely. "Guinevere was one

full-blood magick and her gifts were prodigious. How is it that she died as mortals do?"

I wasn't about to give her my family history while the man I love was a statue standing next to me.

"I am no longer a child, Rohesia, and I am no longer without magick. Undo the spell or I will—"

"We are of the same beginnings. A marriage between your clan and mine will secure the future for all. There is great strength in unity."

"You'd be a lot more convincing if you hadn't turned out our lights, magicked Sugar Maple into a statue garden, and wrapped one of your own in chains."

Okay, so maybe I'd gone too far.

Her enormous eyes blazed red as her robes. The cloud or mist or fog or whatever it was that surrounded her spread across the sky, claiming it as her own. She cursed me in pungent, albeit archaic, terms, her voice rising in pitch and volume like an out-of-control burglar alarm from hell. Words spilled from her beautiful lips, ugly words filled with hate and more than a touch of fear. A rumble of thunder was followed by a crack of lightning and an ominous feeling of impending doom.

"Take the baby!" I quickly handed Laria over to Wendy. "I'm going to—"

Too late.

Rohesia launched a shimmering silver thunderbolt toward me and in that same instant my baby sorceress tore free from Wendy's grasp and launched her tiny but powerful self toward Rohesia with every ounce of magick at her command.

Rohesia moved swiftly to deflect the incoming missile.

Laria slammed into an invisible wall, cried out, then tumbled helplessly toward the ground.

I was fast but Wendy was faster. She grabbed for the baby, couldn't quite connect, but somehow cushioned her fall with her own body.

"She's fine," Wendy called out after an anxious moment. "I've got her!"

Relief coupled with gratitude is a potent mix. It almost undid me. I struggled to regroup.

"You have gone too far, Rohesia!" Gavan, still in chains, roared. "That child is the key to our future!"

The chains rattled as they tightened around Gavan's body but his face gave away nothing.

"Put aside your fears and prejudices, Rohesia," he ordered, "and listen to what I say. This isn't the world you know. This world is bigger and far better than anything we imagined but there is no place for us here if we can't change. Magicks are a small percentage of this dimension. It is a mortal world and it is up to us to figure out how to live among them and honor their ways."

"Gavan and I don't need to marry in order to bring our families together," I said, not entirely sure I wanted to throw Sugar Maple's fate in with this lot. "There are other ways."

"You are half human," she said, putting a particularly unpleasant spin on the last word. "Our history shows that humans cannot be trusted."

"Are you blind?" Gavan demanded. "Did you not see the way the mortal Wendy put Laria's safety before her own?"

Rohesia nodded. "I had never before seen a mortal risk anything for a magick."

"And this was not the first time," Gavan continued. He

recounted the story about Laria and the wobbly dresser and how Wendy again saved the baby from peril. (Even if it was Elspeth-inspired peril.)

Wendy was shaking so hard, I was afraid she'd fall over. "I love her," she said simply. "I would do anything for her and for Chloe and Luke."

I believed her and, from the way Gavan looked at her, I thought he believed her too. Rohesia, however, was a much tougher sell.

But that was Rohesia's problem.

"Laria is more mortal than she is magick," I reminded Rohesia, "but her powers already exceed mine."

"A new world demands a new way of living," Gavan said. "We have much to learn but with Chloe's help, we can make the transition in harmony with Sugar Maple."

She said nothing. Her image faded until it was more memory than reality and as it did, the chains dropped away from him. Way to end the conversation, Rohesia.

"She is considering her options," Gavan said, kicking them away. "She is not a foolish woman. She will see that I am right."

"I'm not so sure," I said. "The woman wrapped you in chains."

"She is the mother of my mother," he said with a quick approximation of a smile. "She will not harm me. She believes magick should never harm magick."

"She tried to harm me," I reminded him. "And the baby."

He had no answer for that.

"Our time runs out," he said. "In less than ten earth days our clan will pierce the veil unless we can find a home in this dimension."

"And she just figured this out?"

"The death of our dimension had been steady and slow over centuries. We thought we had time to unite our clans before it happened but in the last few earth months its progress has accelerated."

"If we were betrothed as children, why did Rohesia wait so long to force us to marry?"

"As I said, time moves more slowly in our dimension. When the blueflame warning all magicks to avoid the Spirit Trail until after your wedding reached us, Rohesia realized she had to take immediate action or all would be lost. When the ring was activated, we knew where to find you."

I held up my hand, the one with the blinking ring on it. "I don't want to marry you," I said.

"I do not wish to marry you either. You are already wed in all the ways that matter. I will not divide a family."

"You understand that so why doesn't she?"

"We have lived in isolation since the separation of the clans. Our way of life was established centuries ago and is deeply ingrained in Rohesia and the Elders. Some of us have traveled between dimensions and have returned with stories of amity between mortals and magicks that are viewed with great suspicion."

"A little suspicion isn't necessarily a bad thing. Life here is good for magicks but it isn't perfect."

He looked at me and smiled one of those Fae smiles that can bring any woman, mortal or magick, to her knees. "You give me hope, Chloe of Guinevere."

"Sorry for interrupting," Wendy said, glancing from me to Gavan, "but Laria wants her mommy."

The baby was squirming in Wendy's arms, making little

sounds of frustration as she reached out in my general direction.

"It was you," Wendy said to him, a touch of aggression in her tone. "You're the guy who knocked me over in front of Sticks & Strings."

He didn't deny it.

"Where's that fabulous embroidered cloak?" she asked.

"The day is hot. I left it at the waterfall."

So he had already discovered the waterfall and, more than likely, the portals the waterfall concealed.

Wendy didn't back down. "Next time you might want to say you're sorry."

Their eyes locked and for a moment I felt like a fifth wheel.

It turned out the baby didn't want me. She wanted her daddy. She poked him in his arm with a chubby finger. She made noises that were just on the verge of being actual words. She aimed her best toothless smile in his direction but he just wasn't there.

And then she began to cry. All the magick at her command (and that was considerable) wasn't bringing her daddy back to her and it was clear her heart was breaking. In the silence of Proctor Park, her cries were heart-wrenching.

"Do something," I said to Gavan. "You understand Rohesia's magick. Try to undo the spell."

I guess that got Rohesia's attention because, just like that, she was no longer in the faded cloud; she was there among us, tall and resplendent in carnelian red robes shot through with silver threads. I wasn't sure if she was real or a hologram but it didn't matter. Her powers were strong and they poured from her in waves. But they were different from the powers at work in our world and at odds with much of the wonders the mortals had wrought into existence since she last walked in our dimension.

A major disturbance in the force, for sure.

Part of me wanted to unleash every micron of magick at my command and blow Rohesia away for trying to harm Laria, but I knew I had to be careful. Until she undid whatever unholy magick she had used to freeze-frame Luke and our wedding guests, I needed to hold my fire. We might not be so lucky next time.

None of us said a word. I wasn't sure we were breathing. I wiggled my finger, just to make sure we hadn't become statues too.

Laria, however, abruptly stopped crying and turned her attention from Luke to the magnificent female standing before us. Laria's huge golden eyes widened as she studied the beautiful Fae with an intensity that quite frankly made me a little nervous. She was only eight months old but there was definitely a very old and very wise soul at work inside that chubby body. (Not to mention more magick than I will ever possess in my lifetime.) She was also unpredictable and impulsive, courtesy of her mother.

Rohesia stood very still and allowed the scrutiny. I sensed a slight softening of her expression as the newest Hobbs sorceress boldly took her measure.

I was both scared and proud when Laria held out her arms to Rohesia in the classic baby human request to be held.

Rohesia hesitated.

Her eyes met mine.

I shook my head.

"I don't trust you," I said. "You tried to hurt my child."

"It was a terrible mistake in judgment," she said. "I am ashamed. Magick should never harm magick. My anger overflowed."

"How do I know it won't happen again?"

"You don't," Rohesia said. "All you can do is trust that it will not. I give you my word."

"And will you trust the mortals who are part of our lives and help keep them safe from harm as well?"

"I will learn. Gavan has made it clear that there can be no other way."

I glanced over at Gavan. Hard to imagine Rohesia baking up a batch of chocolate chip cookies for the grandkids. I wondered if she knew how to knit.

"This is my wedding day." I felt myself growing stronger with every word. "You will undo the spell you cast on my friends and family. You will free Gavan and me from the betrothal. Luke and I will marry as planned." I took a deep breath and plunged into the deep end of a very murky pool. "And tomorrow you and Gavan and I will talk about reuniting our clans."

Rohesia had been a leader for a very long time. She was used to being the Alpha dog in the pack. But here in Sugar Maple there was only one leader and it wasn't Rohesia. She needed to understand that up front. We both did.

I watched quietly as Rohesia's gaze traveled the expanse of Proctor Park where the wedding was taking place. She took it all in: the mortals and the magicks; the young and the old; the humans I loved and the two who shared my blood.

I didn't want to open up our little town to an Old Magick clan of strangers but I had no choice. Their lives were at stake and Aerynn had established Sugar Maple as a refuge for magicks in peril. Turning Rohesia and her community away was not an option.

She was frightened. I saw that now. Everything she knew, everything she understood, was about to be stripped from her as she led her clan into a strange new world. She needed to find the strength to lead and to inspire. But first she had to learn our ways and make them her own. Otherwise, the future looked bleak.

Gavan appeared at my side and we held up our hands to her.

"Release us," he said. "Take the first step into our future."

The rings blazed with light, flickered, then opened wide so we could slip them off. I handed mine to Gavan.

"For when the right one comes along," I said. I tried not to notice the quick glance he stole at Wendy.

"We will stay to observe but not participate." Rohesia paused, then added, "With your permission."

I appreciated how much that cost her. "Of course," I said. "In a few days, this will be your home too."

"There is much to learn," she said with a small shake of her head. "Nothing here is as I thought it would be."

"Nothing ever is," I said lightly. "Welcome to Sugar Maple."

Epilogue

CHLOE

"--MY HUSBAND, my partner, my soulmate in good times and bad, in health and in sickness, for now and forever." My voice shook with emotion as I finished pledging my life, my heart, my forever, to Luke.

As promised, Rohesia undid the freeze-spell and it was as if nothing had ever happened. Once again, the sky was sunny and bright. Laughter and excited whispers mingled with bird song.

And the man I loved was about to become my husband.

I didn't think it would matter. I thought we were already married in all the ways that really counted.

I was wrong. Standing here in front of the people we loved and who loved us in return, taking these very private vows for all to hear, was life-changing. Now everyone knew what we had always known: our family was forever.

Cyrus beamed a smile at us as we exchanged rings. "And now it is my honor to declare Luke MacKenzie and Chloe Hobbs forever joined in marriage as witnessed here today by beloved family and friends." He gave Luke a wink. "This might be a good time to kiss the bride, son."

Our crazy, over-the-top, Hollywood-style kiss had everyone cheering as sparks crackled and snapped when our lips met.

"How do we explain that?" Luke asked with a laugh as Elspeth handed a giggling Laria to him.

"We don't," I said, feeling reckless. "Let them chalk it up to love."

"You'll bring me up to speed on things later," Luke said as we started up the aisle.

"How did you know?" I should have realized not even the best magick spell could fool a good cop for long.

"I'm a cop," he said. "And besides, that damn ring is gone."

There was so much to share, so many things to tell him. Our town was going to change over the next week or two and I wasn't convinced the changes would be welcomed with open arms. I would have to call a town meeting tomorrow, after speaking with Rohesia and Gavan, to bring everyone else up to speed. Not exactly the honeymoon most brides dreamed about.

But then again I wasn't most brides.

I was Chloe Hobbs. Sorceress. Knitter. Wife of Luke MacKenzie. Mother of Laria. Cousin of Wendy. Sister-of-the-heart to Janice and Lynette and Lilith who always had my back.

And I was getting stronger every day.

Coming June 15, 2018

ENTANGLED - THE HOMECOMING

When a young mother and her baby daughter go missing during an early snowstorm, Sugar Maple is suddenly thrust into the spotlight. If Luke and his squad of magickal deputies can't locate them ASAP, Sugar Maple will be Ground Zero for every news organization in the country.

And it couldn't be happening at a worse time. Rohesia and the Old World magicks are making the transition to the earthly dimension and it isn't going smoothly.

Hiding in plain sight had never been more dangerous.

Hungry news crews are poised to overrun Sugar Maple as the search for the missing hikers intensifies. They're looking for the next big story but little do they know the one they uncover just might be the biggest story of the century.

The Sugar Maple Chronicles - Book 6

The Secret Language of Knitting

The knitting vocabulary can be confusing to civilians (a.k.a. muggles) so here's a short glossary to help get you up to speed.

BIND OFF - See "cast off"

BSJ - Baby Surprise Jacket, probably EZ's most popular design

CAST OFF - To secure your last row of stitches so they don't unravel

CAST ON - To place a foundation row of stitches on your needle

DPN - Double-pointed needles

EZ - Elizabeth Zimmermann, the knitting mother of us all

FAIR ISLE - Multistranded colorwork

FO - Finished object

FROG - To undo your knitting by ripping back ("Rip it! Rip it!") row by row with great abandon

KITCHENER - Grafting two parallel rows of live stitches to form an invisible seam

KNIT - The basic stitch from which everything derives

KNITALONG - An online phenomenon wherein hundreds of knitters embark on a project simultaneously and exchange progress reports along the way

KUREYON - A wildly popular self-striping yarn created and manufactured by Eisaku Noro under the Noro label

LYS - Local yarn shop

MAGIC LOOP - Knitting a tube with one circular needle instead of four or five double-pointed needles

PURL - The knit stitch's sister—instead of knitting into the back of the stitch with the point of the needle facing away from you, you knit into the front of the stitch with the point of the needle facing directly at you

RAVELRY - An online community for knitters and knitwear designers that has surpassed all expectations

ROVING - What you have after a fleece has been washed, combed, and carded; roving is then ready to be spun into yarn

SABLE - Stash Amassed Beyond Life Expectancy—in other words, you won't live long enough to knit it all!

SEX - Stash Enhancement eXercise—basically spending too much money on way too much yarn

STASH - The yarn you've been hiding in the empty oven, clean trash bins, your basement, your attic, under the beds, in closets, wherever you can keep your treasures clean, dry, and away from critical eyes

STITCH 'N' BITCH - A gathering of like-minded

knitters who share knitting techniques and friendship with a twenty-first-century twist

STRANDED - See "Fair Isle"

TINK - To carefully undo your knitting stitch by stitch. Basically to unknit your way back to a mistake-free area

YARN CRAWL - The knitter's equivalent of a pub crawl. Substitute yarn shops for bars and you'll get the picture

Who's Who in Sugar Maple

THE RESIDENTS

CHLOE HOBBS - The half-human, half-sorceress de facto mayor of Sugar Maple and owner of Sticks & Strings, a wildly successful knit shop. As the descendant of sorceress Aerynn, the town's founder, Chloe holds the fate of the magickal town in her hands.

LUKE MACKENZIE - The 100 percent human chief of police. He came to Sugar Maple to investigate the death of Suzanne Marsden, an old high school friend, but stayed because he fell in love with Chloe.

PYEWACKET, BLOT, DINAH, LUCY - Chloe's house cats.

PENELOPE - Chloe's store cat. Penny is actually much more than that. She has been a familiar of the Hobbs women for over three centuries and has often served as a conduit between dimensions.

ELSPETH - A three-hundred-something-year-old troll

from Salem who kept house for Samuel Bramford. She has been sent to Sugar Maple to watch over Chloe until the baby is born.

JANICE MEANY - Chloe's closest friend and owner of Cut & Curl, the salon across the street from Sticks & Strings. Janice is a Harvard-educated witch, descended from a long line of witches. She and her husband, Lorcan, have five children.

LORCAN MEANY - Janice's husband. Lorcan is a selkie and one of Luke's friends.

LYNETTE PENDRAGON - A shifter and owner, with her husband, Cyrus, of Sugar Maple Arts Players. They have five children: Vonnie, Iphigenia, Troy (originally named Gilbert), Adonis (originally named Sullivan), and Will.

LILITH - A Norwegian troll who is Sugar Maple's town librarian and historian. She is married to Archie. Her mother was Sorcha the Healer, who cared for Chloe after her parents died.

MIDGE STALLWORTH - A rosy-cheeked vampire who runs the funeral home with her husband, George.

RENATE WEAVER - Member of the Fae and owner of the Sugar Maple Inn. Renate and her husband, Colm, have four grown children: Bettina, Daisy, Penelope, and Calliope.

BETTINA WEAVER LEONIDES - Harpist, member of the Fae, occasional part-time worker at Sticks & Strings. Married to Alexander. Mother of three children: Memphis, Athens, Ithaca.

PAUL GRIGGS - Werewolf and owner of Griggs Hardware. He is Luke's closest friend in town. He is married to Verna and has two sons: Jeremy and Adam. His nephew Johnny is a frequent visitor.

FRANK - One of the more garrulous vampire retirees at Sugar Maple Assisted Living.

MANNY - Another vampire retiree who pals around with Frank.

ROSE - Frank's and Manny's love interest. She is also a retired vampire who resides at Sugar Maple Assisted Living.

SAMUEL - A four-hundred-plus-year-old wizard who pierced the veil at the end of *Spun by Sorcery*. He was Aerynn's lover and the father of the Hobbs clan.

SORCHA - The healer who stayed behind in the mortal world to raise Chloe to adulthood after her parents died in a car crash. Sorcha is Lilith's birth mother.

AERYNN - A powerful sorceress from Salem who led the magickal creatures from Salem to freedom during the infamous Witch Trials. A gifted spinner, she founded Sinzibukwud in northern Vermont (later renamed Sugar Maple) and passed her magick and her spinning and knitting skills down to generations of Hobbs women. Aerynn is responsible for the magick charm that enables Sugar Maple to hide in plain sight.

GUINEVERE - Chloe's sorceress mother. Guinevere chose to pierce the veil after the auto accident that took her beloved husband's life.

TED AUBRY - Chloe's human father and Guinevere's husband. He was a carpenter by trade. Ted was in medical school when he met Guinevere but gave it up to be with her. A very romantic story until Chloe learned her mother had cast a spell on him to bind him to her.

ISADORA - The most powerful member of the Fae.

She is also the most dangerous. Currently Isadora is banished from this realm until the end of time but who knows what the future might bring.

GUNNAR - The good twin, he sacrificed himself so Chloe and Luke could be together.

DANE - The ultimate evil twin.

THE HARRIS FAMILY - They were carpenters in life (c. 1860) but now inhabit the spirit world.

THE SOUDERBUSH BOYS - Father Benjamin, mother Amelia, and sons David, William, and John are all ghosts who spend a lot of time on the Spirit Trail, which passes through the Sugar Maple Inn.

SIMONE - A seductive spirit who specializes in breaking up happy marriages. She usually manifests herself in a wisteria-scented lilac cloud.

FORBES THE MOUNTAIN GIANT - His name pretty much says it all.

THE NEW NEIGHBORS

ROHESIA OF OLWYN – Leader of a clan of Others who have lived for centuries in a dimension beyond the mist that has reached the end of its natural life.

GAVAN OF ERES – Rohesia's grandson. He is a warrior who was betrothed to Chloe when they were children. He was sent to Sugar Maple to stop her marriage to Luke.

CHLOE'S COUSIN

WENDY AUBRY LATTIMER – A second cousin (a few times removed) via Chloe's human father Ted Aubry. She is young, divorced, and a great knitter.

THE MACKENZIE CLAN

BUNNY - Matriarch, knitter, retired nurse. Born and raised in the Boston suburbs near Salem.

JACK - Patriarch, sport fisherman, retired welder. Also born and raised in the Boston suburbs near Salem.

RONNIE - A successful Realtor, father of four. Married to Denise. He still lives in the town where he was born and raised.

KIMBERLY - Luke's oldest sister. Kim is a financial analyst, married, mother of one with husband Travis Davenport. They have been married nine years. She and Chloe formed an easy bond right from the start.

JENNIFER - Another of Luke's older sisters. She's married to Paul and mother of Diandra, Sean, and Colin.

KEVIN - Luke's younger brother. He has been married to Tiffany for nine years. They have four children: Ami, Honor, Scott, and Michael.

PATRICK - Another younger brother. He's newly divorced from Siobhan. They have two daughters: Caitlin and Sarah.

MEGHAN - The wild card of the bunch. Meghan is the youngest of Bunny and Jack's children and the least predictable. (Her two-minutes younger twin died at birth.) She has the habit of taking up with the wrong guys and paying for it with a broken heart.

FRAN KELLY - Retired administrative assistant to Boston's police chief. Close friend of the MacKenzie family.

STEFFIE - Luke's daughter, who was six years old when she died in a bicycle accident.

KAREN - Luke's ex-wife, who sacrificed herself to save their daughter's soul.

JOE RANDAZZO - County Board of Supervisors; a politician who is an occasional thorn in Chloe's side.

Message from Barbara

Readers are everything.

Seeing your name in print is terrific. Good reviews put a smile on an author's face.

Royalties help keep the wolf from the door. But the absolute best thing about being a writer is being read.

Knowing that your words are making someone you're not even related to happy. Knowing that your story is helping to make a bad day better for a stranger who needed to escape for a few hours. Knowing that the imaginary friends you've spent the last few months with are out there in the world becoming just as real to a reader you'll never meet but know and love just the same.

See what I mean?

Readers are everything.

So this one is for the wonderful readers (and knitters) who have taken time over the last few years to let me know how much they enjoy my books.

Thank you from the bottom of my heart.

And if you're new to my work, welcome. I hope you'll check out these other titles and excerpts and let me know what you think.

Happy reading!

Barbara Bretton

Also by Barbara Bretton

Collections - Anthologies

Now and Forever: The Complete Crosse Harbor Trilogy

Happily Ever After: Three Complete Romances

Happily Ever After 2: Five Complete Romances

Home Front: Three novels of love, war, and family

The Rocky Hill Holiday Collection: Two novels and two novellas

Untamed Hearts: Three complete historical romances

Second Time Around: Two wedding novellas

The PAX Collection – 4 novels of romance and adventure

The Sugar Maple Chronicles – 4 books

The Wilde Sisters

Operation: Husband

Operation: Baby

Operation: Family (not yet released)

Bachelor Fathers

Daddy's Girl

The Bride Came C.O.D.

The Crosse Island Harbor Time Travel Trilogy

Somewhere in Time

Tomorrow & Always

Destiny's Child

Someone Like You

Shelter Rock Cove

A Soft Place to Fall

Girls of Summer

Home Front

Where or When

Sentimental Journey

Stranger in Paradise

Historical Romances

Midnight Lover

Fire's Lady

Reluctant Bride

Novellas

I Do, I Do... Again

The Marrying Man

Jersey Strong Novels

The Day We Met

Once Around

Sleeping Alone

Maybe This Time

Just Like Heaven

Just Desserts

Classic Romances

About the Author

Barbara Bretton is the USA Today bestselling, award-winning author of more than 50 books. She currently has over ten million copies in print around the world. Her works have been translated into twelve languages in over twenty countries and she has received starred reviews from both *Publishers Weekly* and *Booklist*. Many of her titles are also available in audio.

Barbara has been featured in articles in *The New York Times, USA Today, Wall Street Journal, Romantic Times, Cleveland Plain Dealer, Herald News, Home News, Somerset Gazette*, among others, and has been interviewed by Independent Network News Television, appeared on the Susan Stamberg Show on NPR, and been featured in an interview with Charles Osgood of WCBS, among others.

Her awards include both Reviewer's Choice and Career Achievement Awards from Romantic Times; a RITA nomination from RWA, Gold and Silver certificates from Affaire de Coeur; the RWA Region 1 Golden Leaf; and several sales awards from Bookrak. Ms. Bretton was included in a recent edition of Contemporary Authors.

When she's not writing, Barbara can be found knitting, cooking, or reading.

She lives in New Jersey with her husband and a houseful of pets.

To subscribe to Barbara's infrequent newsletter, click here.

Excerpt from Casting Spells

In case you're new to Sugar Maple and would like to catch up with all that went before, here's a free look at the first chapter of the first book in the series, *Casting Spells*.

CHLOE

Sugar Maple, Vermont

Do you ever wonder why things happen the way they do? All of those seemingly random decisions we make throughout our lives that turn out to be not so random after all. Maybe if I had closed the shop twenty minutes earlier that night or gone for a quick walk around Snow Lake, she might still be alive today.

But I didn't and that choice changed our lives forever.

At the moment when it all began, I was down on my knees, muttering ancient curses under my breath as I tugged, pulled, and tried to convince five feet of knitted lace that it would be much happier stretched out to six plus.

If there were any magic spells out there to help a girl block a shawl I hadn't found them, and believe me, I'd looked. Blocking, like life, was equal parts intuition, brute strength, and dumb luck.

(Just in case you were wondering, I usually don't mention the dumb luck part when I give a workshop.)

That Monday night I was two hours into Blocking 101, teaching my favorite techniques to three yarn-crawling sisters from Pennsylvania, a teacher from New Jersey, and a retired rocket scientist from Florida. We had been expecting a busload of fiber fanatics from northern Maine, but a wicked early winter blizzard had stopped them somewhere west of Bangor. Two of my best friends from town, admitted knit shop groupies and world-class gossips, rounded out the class.

By the way, I'm Chloe Hobbs, owner of Sticks & Strings, voted the number one knit shop in New England two years running. I don't know exactly who did the voting, but I owe each of those wonderful knitters some quiviut and a margarita. Blog posts about the magical store in northern Vermont where your yarn never tangles, your sleeves always come out the same length, and you always, always get gauge were popping up on a daily basis, raising both my profile and my bottom line.

Sometimes I worried that this sudden, unexpected burst of fame and fortune had extended the tourist season beyond the town's comfort zone. Hiding in plain sight was harder than it sounded, but for now our secret was still safe.

A blocking board was spread open on the floor. A dark blue Spatterware bowl of T-pins rested next to it. My trusty spray bottle of warm water had been refilled twice. I probably looked like a train wreck as I crawled my way around the perimeter, pinning each scallop and point into position, but those were the breaks.

Since blocking lace was pretty much my only cardio these days, when the wolf whistle sailed overhead, I didn't bother to look up.

"Wow!" Janice Meany, owner of Cut & Curl across the street, murmured. "Those can't be real."

If I'd had any doubt about the wolf whistles, Janice's statement erased it. Last I heard, not too many women were ordering 34As from their neighborhood cosmetic surgeon.

"Implants," Lynette Pendragon declared in a voice that could be heard in the upper balcony of her family's Sugar Maple Arts Playhouse. "Or a really good wizard."

It was times like this when I wished I had inherited a tiny bit of magick from my mother. Just enough to render my indiscreet friend speechless for a second or two. Everyone in Sugar Maple knows we don't talk about wizards in front of civilians unless the conversation includes Munchkins and Oz.

Fortunately our guests had other things on their minds. "I'm glad my Howie isn't here," one of the Pennsylvania sisters breathed. "She looks like Sharon Stone. Howie has a thing for Sharon Stone."

"Sharon Stone fifteen years ago on a good day," the New Jersey schoolteacher added. "A very good day."

What can I say? I'm only a human. (And a nosy one at that.) I dumped the lace and glanced toward the front window.

Winter comes early to our part of Vermont. By the time the last of the leaf-peepers have headed down to the lesser glories of New York and Connecticut, we're digging out our snowshoes and making sure our woodpiles are well stocked.

In mid-December it's dark and seriously cold by four thirty, and only the most intrepid window-shopping tourist would ever consider strolling down Main Street without at least five layers of clothing.

The woman peering in at us was blond, tall, and around my age, but that was where the resemblance ended. I'm the kind of woman who could disappear into a crowd even if her hair was on fire. Our window shopper couldn't disappear if she tried. Her movie-star-perfect face was pressed up against the frosty glass and we had a full-frontal glimpse of bare arms, bare shoulders, and cleavage that would send Pamela Anderson running back to her surgeon.

"Am I nuts or is she naked?" I asked no one in particular.

"I think she's strapless," Janice said, but she didn't sound convinced.

"It can't be more than ten degrees out there," one of the Pennsylvanians said, exchanging looks with her sisters. "She must be crazy."

"Or drunk," Lynette offered.

"I'll bet she was mugged," the rocket scientist volunteered. "I saw a weird-looking guy lurking down the block when I parked my car."

I was tempted to tell her that the weird-looking guy was a half-asleep vampire named Buster on an ice cream run for his pregnant wife, but I figured that might not be good for business.

The possibly naked woman at the window tapped twice, mimed a shiver, then pointed toward the locked door, where the CLOSED sign was prominently displayed.

"Are you going to make her stand out there all night?" Janice asked. "Maybe she needs help."

She definitely isn't here for a new set of double points, I thought as I flipped the lock. Not that I profile my customers or anything, but I'd bet my favorite rosewoods that she had never cast on a stitch in her life and intended to keep it that way.

My second thought as she swirled past me into the shop was, Wow, she really is naked. It took a full second for me to realize that was an illusion created by a truly gifted dressmaker with access to spectacular yard goods.

My third thought--well, I didn't actually have a third thought. I was still working on the second one when she smiled at me and somewhere out there a dentist counted his T-bills.

"I'm Chloe," I said as I looked into her sea green eyes. Eyes like that usually came with magical powers (and more than a little bit of family history), but she had the vibe of the pure human about her. "I own the shop."

"Suzanne Marsden." She extended a perfectly manicured hand and I thought I caught a shiver of Scotch on her breath. "I think you might have saved my life."

"Literally or figuratively?" I asked.

I've dealt with lots of life-or-death emergencies at Sticks & Strings, but most of them included dropped stitches and too many margaritas at our Wednesday Night Knit-Ins.

She laughed as Janice and Lynette exchanged meaningful looks I tried very hard to ignore.

"I can't believe they wouldn't seat me early at the Inn. I thought I could flirt with the bartender until my boyfriend arrived but no such luck."

It was probably the first time anyone had ever refused her anything, and she looked puzzled and annoyed in an amused kind of way.

"The Weavers can be a tad rigid," I said, studiously avoiding eye contact with my townie friends, who knew exactly why the Weavers acted the way they did. "I promise you the food's worth the aggravation."

"I left my coat in the car so I could make a big sweeping Hollywood entrance, and now I not only can't get into the damn restaurant, I locked myself out of my car and would probably have frozen to death out there if you hadn't taken pity on me and opened your door."

"Honey, you're in Vermont," Janice said. "You can't go around like that up here. You'll freeze your nipples off."

"She said she has a coat," I reminded Janice a tad sharply. As a general rule I find it best not to discuss politics, religion, or my customer's nipples in the shop. "It's locked in her car."

"With my cell and my skis and my ice skates," Suzanne said with a theatrical eye roll. "All I need is to use your phone so I can call Triple A."

"Oh, don't bother with them," Lynette said with a wave of her hand. "They'll take all night to get up here. My daughter Vonnie can have it open in a heartbeat."

Suzanne's perfectly groomed right eyebrow rose slightly. "If it's not too much trouble, that would be great."

Clearly she thought Vonnie was majoring in grand theft auto at Sugar Maple High, but that was a whole lot better than telling her that the teenager could make garage doors roll open three towns away just by thinking about them.

There were some things tourists were better off not knowing.

I shot Lynette a look. "So you're going to go call Vonnie now, right?"

We both knew she had already put out the call to her

daughter, but we're all about keeping up appearances here in Sugar Maple.

"I'm on it," Lynette said and went off in search of her cell phone.

I turned back to our visitor, who was up to her elbows in a basket of angora roving waiting to be spun into yarn, while Penelope, the ancient store cat who shared the basket, ignored her.

"This is glorious. I've thought about learning to knit but--" She shrugged. "You know how it is."

Well, not really. I've been knitting since I was old enough to hold a pair of needles.

"I'll be spinning that next week," I told her while we waited for Lynette to return, "then knitting it up into a shawl."

She wandered to the stack of shawls on the shelf and fingered a kid silk Orenburg I had on display. "Don't tell me you made this?"

"Chloe knitted everything in the shop," Janice volunteered.

"Impossible!" Suzanne Marsden looked over at me. "Did you really? I love handmade garments and this is heirloom quality."

She might have been lying through her porcelain veneers but it was all the encouragement I needed. I whipped out the Orenburg and was treated to the kind of adulation usually reserved for rock stars.

"Amazing," Suzanne breathed as I laid the shawl across her slender shoulders. "You couldn't possibly have made this without divine intervention."

I started to spout my usual it's-all-just-knit-and-purl shop owner spiel when to my surprise the truth popped out instead. "It almost put me into intensive care," I admitted to the background laughter of my friends, "but I made it to the other side."

And then I showed her the trick that either sent prospective knitters running back to their crochet hooks or won them over forever. I slipped my mother's wedding band off my right forefinger and passed the shawl through the small circle of Welsh gold.

"How much?" Suzanne asked.

"It's not for sale," Lynette answered before I had the chance to open my mouth. "Chloe never sells her Orenburgs."

"In my experience there are exceptions to every absolute." Suzanne favored me with a smile that was a half-degree away from flirtatious. "Name your price."

"Dangerous words to use in front of a shop owner," I said lightly, "but Lynette is right. The shawls on that shelf are for display only."

Suzanne met my eyes, and I saw something behind the smile that took me by surprise.

Pretty people aren't supposed to be sad. Isn't that the story you were told when you were a little girl? Pretty people are supposed to get a free ride through this life and possibly the next one too.

That was the thing about running a shop. Every now and then a customer managed to push the right buttons and my business sense, shaky at the best of times, went up in smoke.

I swiped her platinum AmEx through the machine and slid the receipt across the counter for her signature.

"Would you like me to wrap it for you?" I asked while Lynette and Janice kept the other customers amused.

"No, thanks," she said, pirouetting in front of the cheval mirror in the corner. "I'll wear it."

Lynette popped back in. "Vonnie texted me," she said to Suzanne. "Your car's unlocked and the Inn is open for business."

Suzanne flashed us a conspiratorial grin. "My boyfriend always keeps me waiting. It wouldn't hurt him to do a little waiting himself."

But she didn't keep him waiting long. She signed her receipt, made a few polite noises, then hurried back out into the darkness.

"I'd give anything to see the boyfriend," one of the Pennsylvania sisters said after the door clicked shut behind Suzanne Marsden. "I'll bet we're talking major hottie."

"Johnny Depp hot or George Clooney hot?" the schoolteacher from New Jersey asked, and everyone laughed.

The rocket scientist gave out a cross between a snicker and a snort. "That woman has future trophy wife written all over her. Odds are he's old, wrinkled, and rich."

"Maybe she loves him," I said then immediately wished I'd kept my big mouth shut.

Janice and Lynette exchanged glances and I didn't need extrasensory powers to know exactly what they were thinking. I shot them my best "don't you dare" warning look. One thing I didn't need was another lecture on love from Sugar Maple's two most dangerous matchmakers.

Blocking lace seemed a little anticlimactic to me after Suzanne's mini-drama. I was seriously tempted to excuse myself for a minute then race up the street so I could peek through the front window of the Inn and eyeball the guy she was meeting, but that wasn't how Sticks & Strings had maintained its ranking as the number one knit shop in New England two years running.

So I stayed put, but that didn't mean I was happy about it.

It was a little before ten by the time everyone exchanged names and phone numbers and e-mail addresses. I handed out goodie bags of knitting gadgets and yarn samples and smiled at the oohs and ahhs of appreciation. Welcome to the dark side, ladies. Before long they would need an extra room to house their stash.

I let out a loud sigh of relief as I sank into one of the over-stuffed chairs near the Ashford wheels. "I actually broke into a sweat blocking that shawl." I flapped the hem of my T-shirt for emphasis.

Janice rolled her eyes. "You're not going to get any sympathy from me. Try giving a full body wax to an over-weight eighty-five-year-old man with more wrinkles than a shar-pei. Now that's a workout."

Too much information. What went on behind the closed doors of Cut & Curl was none of my business.

"Seriously. I thought that shawl was going to get the better of me."

"Our visitor is the one who got the better of you," Lynette said. "You barely recouped the cost of the yarn."

Lynette was always trying to give me business advice, and I was always doing my best to ignore her. "I thought we had a great group tonight. Definitely better than the carload of mystery writers who drove in for the finishing workshop last month. Now that was a big mistake."

Leave it to mystery writers to wonder why the Inn flashed a NO OCCUPANCY sign but didn't have any visitors.

"I'm talking about the shawl. She practically stole it from you." Lynette could be like a dog with a stack of short ribs.

"Don't exaggerate."

"You must have spent twice that on yarn."

"I didn't spend anything. That was hand-spun from my mother's stash." When my mother died, one of the things she left me was a basket of roving that remained full to over-flowing no matter how many hours I spent at my wheel, and another was a love of all things fiber.

"Good gods," Lynette shrieked. "It's worse than I thought."

"I'm not crazy," I said, slightly annoyed. "Lilith checks the roving twice a year to make sure it's free from any traveling spells."

Lynette was mollified, but just barely. "You really should drive down to Brattleboro and take a class in small business management," she went on. "Cyrus said it's the best money we ever spent."

Lynette and Cyrus were owners/operators of the Sugar Maple Arts Playhouse at the corner of Carrier Court and Willard Grove. Cyrus was one of the SMAP's favorite performers, which, considering the fact that he was a shapeshifter, made casting a snap. Lynette and their daughters Vonnie and Iphigenia were also shapeshifters and had been known to round out Cyrus's repertory company on more than one occasion. Their sons, the unfortunately named Gilbert and Sullivan were occasionally pressed into service too, but Gil and Sully were quickly reaching the age where it would take cash to turn them into orphaned pirates.

"So you'll think about it?" Lynette pressed. "If you sign

up before the end of the year, Cyrus gets a fifty-dollar rebate."

"I'll think about it," I said, "but it's pretty hard to get away these days."

"You don't want to get away," Janice said as she rinsed out the teapot.

"That's right," Lynette observed as she swept crumbs off the worktable and tossed them into the trash. "You're all about the work lately."

"It would do you good to take a little trip." Janice reached for the coffeepot. "I can't remember the last time you went away for a night or two."

"I can," Lynette said as she fluffed up the pillows on the leather sofa near the fireplace. "It was when she was seeing that lawyer from New Hampshire."

Janice frowned. "That has to be--what? Four, five years ago?"

"Almost six," I said, "and I don't want to talk about it."

"You can't possibly still blame us for that."

"Putting a spell on our car wasn't very funny. We could have frozen to death up there in the woods."

"We moved the relationship along," Lynette broke in. "You should be grateful."

"Lynnie's right," Janice said. "We saved you from making a terrible mistake."

"Howard was handsome, smart, and independently wealthy. Where's the mistake in that?"

"He was human," Janice said. "It wouldn't have worked."

"I'm human," I reminded her.

"Only half," Lynette said. "Your mother was a sorceress."

"Yes, she was, but we all know I take after my father." I had his height, his hair, and his humanness. There wasn't the slightest bit of magick about me and there never had been. I couldn't see into the future or shapeshift or bend spoons with the power of my mind. I was as solid and earth-bound as one of the maple trees in Willard Grove.

"Nothing good happens when magick meets human," Janice went on. "Don't tempt fate, honey. Stick with your own kind."

What they meant was, "Your mother fell in love with a human and see what happened to her."

I was six years old when my parents died in a car crash not far from the Toothaker Bridge. The car skidded on black ice and slammed into a towering maple tree. My human father had been killed instantly. My sorceress mother lingered for two days while Sorcha and Lilith and all the people who loved her did everything in their power to convince her to stay, but in the end Guinevere chose to leave this world to be with the only man she would ever love.

My memories of that time were all in soft focus. Mostly I remember Sorcha, who had opened up her life and her home to me and made me her own.

Sometimes I hated my mother for making that choice. What kind of woman would choose to leave her daughter alone in the world? Depending on the time of day and how much wine I'd consumed, I either found her decision achingly romantic or the act of a supremely selfish woman.

"You're not listening," I said to my friends. "I don't have magick and I probably never will."

"You never know what might happen," Janice said. "You always were a late bloomer. You were the last in your class to start wearing a bra."

I was also the last in my class to score a date to the senior prom, something that still stings even now, thirteen years later. If it hadn't been for my pal Gunnar, I wouldn't have gone at all. "And your point is?"

Lynette leaned forward, all dark-eyed intensity. "My mother told me that your mother didn't come into her full powers until she fell in love."

"But she had some powers before she met my father," I reminded my friends. "I remember the stories. Why can't you both accept the fact that I'm never going to be more than I am right now?"

They exchanged another one of those knowing glances that reminded me of the housewives of Wisteria Lane.

"No matchmaking," I said, barely stifling a yawn. "Absolutely, positively not. I am way too old for matchmaking." Okay, so I was only thirty, but blind dates aged a girl in dog years.

"But he's perfect for you."

"That's what you said about the last one."

Janice had the decency to look a tiny bit sheepish. "I'll admit Jacob was a mistake."

"Jacob was a troll."

Literally.

"Midge Stallworth forgot to mention that. We thought he was vampire like the rest of the family."

"If the Universe wants me to find someone, they'll send me a hot alpaca farmer who likes to spin."

"Honey, you know we're only thinking about your happiness." Lynette patted my hand.

Maybe they were thinking about my happiness, but they were also thinking about the accident just before Christmas last year. A bus carrying a high school hockey team en route to Brattleboro blew a tire and careened down an embankment near the Sugar Maple town limits, killing the goalie and the coach.

Things like that weren't supposed to happen here. Accidents, crime, illness, all the things that plagued every other town in America, didn't happen here. Or at least they hadn't up until recently.

Over three hundred years ago one of my sorcerer ancestors cast a protective charm over the town designed to shield Sugar Maple from harm for as long as one of her line walked the earth and--well, you guessed it. I'm the last descendant of Aerynn, and if you thought your family was on your case to marry and produce offspring, try having an entire town mixing potions, casting runes, and weaving spells designed to hook you up with Mr. Right.

"The accident was random chance," I said, trying to ignore the chill racing up my spine as I remembered the crowd of reporters who had flooded the area. "The weather was terrible. It could have happened anywhere."

"But it didn't happen anywhere," Janice said. "It happened here and it shouldn't have."

"Jan's right," Lynette said. "The spell is growing weaker with every year that passes. I can feel the difference."

Janice nodded. "We all do."

I didn't but that was no surprise. I could only take them at their word on this, same as I did on everything else I couldn't see or hear or understand.

"Cyrus met a charming selkie named Glenn at the Scottish Faire last week," Lynette went on.

"She already dated a selkie," Janice reminded her. "It wasn't a good match."

"I dated a selkie?" The parade of recent losers had mercifully blurred in my memory.

"You said his breath smelled like smoked salmon."

I shuddered. "I'll skip the selkies, thanks."

"You get used to it," Janice, who was married to a selkie, said. "Truth is, you'd skip them all if we let you."

She was right about that.

"Just keep Saturday nights open," Lynette said. "That's all I'm asking."

As far as I could tell, my Saturday nights were open from now until the next millennium. I nodded and stifled another yawn. "No trolls, no selkies," I said. "And he has to be at least six feet tall before the magic kicks in."

"Not a problem," Janice said. "Tall is good."

"Human might be nice for a change."

They looked at me, then at each other, and burst into raucous laughter.

"Honey," Lynette said as she patted my arm, "around here human might not be your best choice."

I wasn't usually prickly about their wariness about humans, but that night it got under my skin. It wasn't like I actually thought Mr. Right was going to show up at Sticks & Strings one snowy winter day searching for the perfect ski sweater to wear on the slopes. But I did think love was possible. It had happened for my parents, hadn't it? Maybe they hadn't managed the happy ending part of the equation, but for a little while I saw what real magic was all about and I didn't want to settle for anything less.

Now you know why I had five cats, one TiVo, and a stash of yarn I couldn't knit my way through in six lifetimes.

I mean, what were the odds that the perfect man would not only show up in Sugar Maple, but also be okay with the fact that the town wasn't the picture-postcard New England town our Chamber of Commerce would have you believe, but a village of vampires, werewolves, elves, faeries, and everything else your parents told you didn't really exist?

Or that he would be okay with the fact that the woman he wanted to spend his life with had a few surprises lurking in her own gene pool?

Ten million to one sounded about right to me.

Besides, Sugar Maple was doing fine without my help. We had a thriving tourist trade and zero crime. What other town could make that claim? It seemed to me that Aerynn's protective blessing was still getting the job done even if we had had a few close calls over the last year or two.

The blessing's strength might be weakening, but we still had time to figure this out before it vanished altogether. All we needed was a frothy little protective charm to cover us until I either found the man of my dreams or came up with a Plan B.

And maybe things would have worked out that way if, just a few hours after she left my shop, Suzanne Marsden hadn't been murdered.

End of Chapter 1

Printed in Great Britain
by Amazon

18028325R00130